LABRADOR in the LEAVES

Ben M. Baglio

Illustrations by Ann Baum

Cover illustration by
Mary Ann Lasher

SCHOLASTIC INC.

New York Toronto London Auckland Sydney
Mexico City New Delhi Hong Kong Buenos Aires

To Nearly-ours, the visitor that stayed

Special thanks to Andrea Abbott

ISBN-13: 978-0-545-06572-6
ISBN-10: 0-545-06572-0

12 11 10 9 8 7 6 5 4 3 2 1   8 9 10 11 12 13/0

Printed in the U.S.A.   40
First Scholastic printing, October 2008

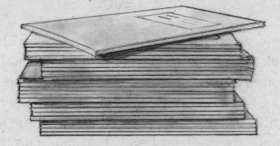

One

"James is going as a jack-o'-lantern," Mandy Hope said to her classmate Susan Collins as they crossed the school yard one Monday morning early in October. They were discussing the upcoming school Halloween party. It was three weeks away, but everyone was already excited about it.

"James the jack-o'-lantern!" Susan chuckled. "That'll be something to see." A gust of wind tugged at her scarf. She grabbed it and tucked the ends inside her jacket. "But how's he going to turn himself into a pumpkin?"

"You mean, without the clock striking midnight?" Mandy joked. She skipped over a twig that had blown down from a nearby oak tree. "Actually, his costume's already half finished," she continued. "He's been working on it all weekend." She started climbing the steps to the entrance foyer. "Last I saw, he'd made a pumpkin-shaped frame that fits over him, right down to his knees. He's going to cover that with an old curtain his mom has dyed orange."

"It sounds like he'll look like a giant lampshade," said Susan.

"Maybe." Mandy grinned, pausing at the front door. "But I think he'll look pretty pumpkinlike, actually." She knew how imaginative James could be. He was eleven, a year younger than her, and they'd been best friends for ages. Mandy's parents, Emily and Adam Hope, owned Animal Ark, a veterinary practice attached to their home in the Yorkshire village of Welford. Hardly a day went by when Mandy and James didn't have to cope with a sick pet or a wild animal in distress. Mandy hadn't met an animal in trouble yet that she hadn't wanted to help — which was fortunate because she had her heart set on becoming a vet, too.

In the foyer, the noise was deafening. It sounded like everyone in the entire school was talking at the same time.

"I'm going as a witch." Mandy overheard Rachel Farmer telling Johnny Pearson. "And Amy's going to be my cat." Amy was Rachel's sister.

"Werewolves are totally cool," Brandon Gill was telling Harriet Ruck.

Susan stopped to ask Brandon about his costume so Mandy walked on alone. She was looking for James. He hadn't been on the bus that morning and she guessed his dad had given him a ride.

There was no sign of him anywhere, even in his classroom, so she continued along the corridor to her own homeroom. Her homeroom teacher, Mr. Clark, was sitting on his desk, talking to a girl Mandy didn't recognize. "Ah, Mandy," he said when he saw her enter. "Come and meet your new classmate, Sara Grant."

Sara turned around. She was nearly as tall as Mandy and had dark blond hair like Mandy's, only longer, which she wore in a high ponytail. Her eyes were hazel colored, and her cheeks were dotted with freckles.

"Welcome to Walton School," Mandy said, smiling. "I hope you'll like it here."

"It looks pretty cool already," said Sara. "Everyone seems like they're really glad it's Monday morning."

Mandy laughed. "That's because of the Halloween party." She glanced at Mr. Clark. "Not because we can't wait to get back to work after the weekend."

"Nonsense! Lessons are a . . . er . . . treat," teased Mr. Clark. He stood up as others started coming in. "But before we have the first big treat of the morning, which, you will remember, is a science test, please help Sara get some supplies. And find her somewhere to sit."

"Sure," said Mandy. She pointed out an empty desk three rows away from her own, dumped her backpack on her chair, then took Sara to the supply cabinet at the back of the room. "How long have you been in Walton?" she asked, opening the doors.

"Four days," said Sara, helping herself to some pens and pencils. "The advertising firm my dad works for transferred him here to open a new office."

Mandy dragged a chair over from the nearest desk. She climbed onto it and reached for a heap of notebooks at the top of the cabinet. She took two and tucked them against her. "Where did you live before?" she asked, jumping down.

"Sherborne," said Sara, as Mandy piled the books into her outstretched arms. "It's in Dorset."

"Oh, right," said Mandy. She knew the pretty rural county of Dorset in the far southwest of England. "Mom and Dad and I were there not so long ago."

"On vacation?" asked Sara.

"Sort of," Mandy said. "More like a working vacation." She thought about the veterinary clinic in the village of

Chaldon Herring that her parents had looked after. In just one week, she'd come across a phantom horse and rider, smugglers, hidden contraband, and endangered giant lizards.

Sara's voice cut into Mandy's thoughts. She was looking puzzled. "What kind of work do your parents do?"

Mandy reached in to the back of the shelf for a pile of loose paper. "They're vets," she said.

"Vets!" exclaimed Sara. "That means I've met exactly the person Mom wanted to contact today."

"Your mom was looking for *me*?" Mandy said in surprise. She put the paper on top of the books in Sara's arms.

"In a way," said Sara. "You see, we need to find a veterinary clinic."

Concerned, Mandy asked, "Is one of your pets ill?"

Sara smiled. "Not at all. But we need to register with a clinic because Shan, our Labrador, has four puppies. They're just six weeks old."

"Labrador puppies!" Mandy exclaimed in delight. She imagined a bundle of plump little dogs, some black, others golden, or even chocolate colored. "They must be adorable."

"They are," said Sara. "You'll have to come and meet them."

"You bet!" Mandy said. She loved making new friends,

but making a new friend who had a dog with puppies was the best sort of Halloween treat!

It was hard to concentrate in class that day. The party fever got worse as the day wore on, with people slipping notes to each other when the teacher's back was turned. Mostly, they were drawings of costumes. Mandy must have received about twenty different sketches, some of them familiar Halloween fare like ghosts and witches, but others were really extraordinary ideas, like her friend Penelope's. She was going to come as the fairy-tale character Rapunzel, wearing a long blond wig and a barrel made from gray poster board that would be the tower. *That would make James's jack-o'-lantern look tame*, Mandy thought.

At last, the final bell rang. Chairs scraped across the floor, lockers banged shut, and the volume of chatter soared as everyone grabbed their bags and headed for the door.

"Homework tonight . . ." Mr. Clark announced.

Silence fell and several dismayed glances flitted across the room.

". . . is to finish your costume designs and *leave them at home*! I don't want to see any more notes making the rounds in my classroom."

Everyone burst out laughing, and Susan Collins said, "You must have eyes in the back of your head, sir."

"Indeed, I do," he said. "We get them made to order at teacher's college."

In the school yard, Mandy spotted James heading for the bicycle rack. It was the first time she'd seen him all day. "Hey, James!" she called, cupping her hands so he could hear her over the wind.

He came over and Mandy introduced him to Sara.

"It's great to meet you at last, James," said Sara, dumping her bag on the ground. It bulged with her new books. "Mandy's told me lots about you."

"None of it's true," he protested with a grin. "I don't eat that much chocolate. Honestly!"

"Oh, yeah?" Mandy challenged. "Actually, I was trying to figure out where you could be. We looked everywhere for you during recess."

James wrinkled his nose. "I was in trouble for being late and missing a test. I had to stay in to finish it."

"Poor you," Mandy said, and saw Sara gave him a sympathetic look, too. "But we've got some news that'll cheer you up."

"What's that?" asked James.

"Sara's Labrador has four puppies."

James's face lit up. "How cool is that!" he exclaimed, then added, "Labradors are the best breed ever."

"You really think so?" said Sara, looking proud.

"I know so," James insisted. "I've got one named Blackie. He's awesome."

"He's also the worst behaved dog in Welford," Mandy put in, grinning.

James looked hurt. "He's just playful."

"Yes, and one of his favorite games is disobeying orders!" Mandy teased.

James made a face to show he knew Mandy was joking, then said, "When can we meet the puppies?"

"We were just going to ask my mom about that," said Sara, heaving her bag over her shoulder.

Mrs. Grant was waiting at the school gate. She looked a lot like Sara, only her hair was short. "It's nice to meet you both," she said to Mandy and James. When Sara explained that Mandy's parents were vets, Mrs. Grant was even more delighted. "That *is* a coincidence," she said. Taking out her cell phone, she asked Mandy for Animal Ark's telephone number. "I want to make an appointment for Shan and the puppies to make sure they're all in perfect health." She programmed in the number and put away the small silver phone. "Maybe you'd like to come and meet the family when your mom or dad visits?"

"I'd love to!" Mandy said, and even though the cold wind whipped around her face and tugged at her jacket, she hardly noticed it. Her thoughts were only of four playful, velvet-soft little Labradors.

"We're about to get five new patients," Mandy told her mom later, when she was helping in the clinic. She was trying to keep an orange-colored cat calm while Dr. Emily cleaned some gashes on his head. The cat, Marble, had been hurt when the wind blew a plastic bag over

his head and he'd hurtled headlong into a holly bush. His owner, an ambulance driver, had rushed him to the clinic, but then was called away immediately to take someone to the hospital.

Dr. Emily dabbed antiseptic on Marble's wounds. "Who are these new patients?"

Mandy told her about Shan and the puppies. "Mrs. Grant is calling later to make an appointment," she said, and winced as Marble's claws sank into her hand. "I think that stuff is really stinging him, Mom." She smoothed him with her other hand. "Sorry, boy, but we have to make sure no germs get in."

After she'd cleaned the cuts, Dr. Emily checked to see if any needed stitching. "Most of them will heal on their own. But I'll have to sew up this gash behind his ear," she said. "We'll give him a rest, though, while I see my other patients." She picked him up and put him into Mandy's arms. He was a friendly cat and he snuggled up against her with his head on her shoulder. "Take him into the residential unit for the time being, please, sweetie," said Dr. Emily.

Mandy had just settled Marble in a cage when the phone rang. She went to answer it but her mom got there first.

"I agree, it's much easier if I come to you rather than you having to bring them all in here," Dr. Emily was saying when Mandy went in to the reception area. "So we'll see you tomorrow at about four thirty." She hung up and turned to Mandy with a smile. "I don't suppose you're remotely interested in coming with me to see Shan and her puppies tomorrow afternoon, are you?" she said.

"Let me see," Mandy said, playing along. "No, not remotely interested. *Very* interested. And I bet James will be, too." She immediately picked up the phone to call James. They were going to meet Shan and the puppies!

The Grants' house was in a new development just outside Walton, the town three miles from Welford where Mandy went to school. It was painted white, and there were bay windows on either side of the front door. It was the last house in a cul-de-sac and had a large yard that backed onto open fields. Beyond the fields was a wooded area that looked perfect for dog walks.

Dr. Emily parked the Land Rover in front of the double garage next to a new white van. Pink flowers were painted on the sides along with a dark green slogan: GORGEOUS GARDENS: LANDSCAPE DESIGN. "The Grants must be having their garden professionally designed," Dr. Emily commented as they climbed out of the Land Rover.

Sara opened the door before they had a chance to ring the doorbell.

"I love your sweater!" Mandy exclaimed. The cozy-looking green knit top was printed with a bright picture of a yellow Labrador.

"Is that Shan?" James asked.

"No. But it looks a little like her," said Sara. "That's why my mom picked it out for me."

Mandy looked past her into the house, hoping to see four lively puppies with their proud mother. Sara must have read her mind. "They're all in the utility room," she said. "Except now we call it the puppy nursery." She led Mandy and her mom and James to the kitchen. Mrs. Grant and a young couple wearing khaki trousers and green sweaters were standing around the table studying a big sheet of paper.

"Dr. Hope and Mandy and James are here," Sara announced.

Mrs. Grant looked up, smiling. "Thank you for agreeing to come out, Dr. Hope."

"No trouble at all," said Dr. Emily. "In fact, it's all Mandy's been talking about since yesterday!"

The young man laughed. He was tall with dark hair and a tanned, pleasant face. "Someone else with nothing but puppies on her mind!" he joked, winking at Sara.

"Oh, I am sorry," said Mrs. Grant. "I haven't introduced everyone." She explained to the young couple who Mandy and her mom and James were. "Faye and Peter Cole are our landscaping team. We were just studying their plans for our yard." She pointed to the paper on the table. "I'm afraid you'll have to excuse me," she apologized to Peter and Faye. "The puppies need to have their first shots."

"Sure," said Faye. She had short, neatly cut blond hair and piercing blue eyes, and she wore diamond ear studs. She was of average height, slight in build, and elegant looking, Mandy thought, for someone whose job was gardening. Flashing a smile at Mandy and James, Faye added, "Those puppies are the cutest you've ever seen."

"The best," agreed Peter. "By the way, I've been meaning to ask you, Barbara, are you a professional dog breeder?"

"No," said Mrs. Grant. "But Shan has a very good pedigree, and a friend of mine who is a top Labrador breeder told us that the puppies are very promising. She said their temperaments are perfect for showing, and their conformation is exceptional."

"Conformation?" Faye echoed, frowning.

"It's how they're built," explained Mrs. Grant. "They have good strong shoulders, straight backs, and well-shaped heads. Even their tails are perfect, apparently — the trademark 'otter tail' of a Labrador."

James nodded in a knowledgeable way. "Short and rounded, with thick hair."

"I see," said Faye, looking impressed. "You must have high hopes for them, Mrs. Grant."

"Indeed, I do."

Peter rolled up the blueprints. "I bet people are lining up to buy them already," he said.

"Just about," said Mrs. Grant. "We ran an advertisement in the *Walton Gazette* the day after we moved in and already the two females have been bought. Of course, we won't be letting any of them go for at least another two weeks. They'll be eight weeks old then, and completely weaned."

"And the males?" asked Faye.

"We've had half a dozen calls about them so far," said Mrs. Grant. "It means we can be very selective about the homes they eventually go to."

"I didn't think you'd have any trouble," said Peter.

Saying good-bye to the landscape designers and leaving them in the kitchen to pack up, Sara and her mom led Mandy and the others to the puppy nursery. Finally, the moment had come; Mandy was going to get her first sight of the Labrador family! When she peered in through the door, she wasn't disappointed. Shan, dark-eyed with glossy golden fur and a gentle, intelligent expression, lay in a roomy box looking very proud. Clambering all over her as if she were a jungle gym were four energetic puppies. Golden-yellow like their mom, chunky in build, and sweet-faced, they were the picture of adorableness.

"They're beautiful!" Mandy breathed. She wanted to rush over and scoop them up for hugs but knew that mother dogs were strongly protective of their young. So she waited at the door with James and her mom. Mrs. Grant stood at the threshold, too, leafing through a folder that was marked SHAN'S PUPPIES.

Sara went in and lifted the puppies out of the box. Kneeling on the ground, she leaned forward while the puppies tumbled in front of her. "Hey! That's my hair!" She laughed when one of them grabbed the end of her ponytail in his teeth and began tugging it. Gently, she pried it from him and looked around.

"Don't you want to meet them?" she said, looking surprised that everyone was still at the door. "They love company, and Shan adores showing them off."

Mandy didn't need a second invitation. She went into the room at once, with James close behind. Shan thumped her tail as if to welcome them, then she licked each puppy in turn. She could have been introducing them to the visitors.

Mandy knew she should greet Shan first to win her confidence. She crouched next to her and stroked her head. "You're a beautiful girl," she said. "And who's this?" she added, patting one of the puppies who wore a yellow ribbon around her neck. The others all wore ribbons, too, each a different color. It was a good way to tell puppies apart when a litter looked identical at first glance.

"That's Tulip," said Sara. She leaned forward and picked her up. "Say hello to Mandy," she said. Kissing the top of the puppy's head, she passed her to Mandy.

"Hi there, Tulip," Mandy said. Tulip stared at her with a trusting expression. She was solid with a round belly, plump from good feeding, and stocky legs. "Aren't you the most gorgeous little dog?" Mandy murmured and held her close, letting Tulip snuggle against her neck. She smelled the familiar milky smell of new puppies, and felt the velvety softness of four little paws resting on her hands. "Her fur's like silk," she said, stroking Tulip's fluffy coat.

"But their teeth are like needles," said James. He had reached for the puppy with the green ribbon and winced when she started treating his fingers like a chew toy.

Mrs. Grant laughed. "Sometimes they're like piranhas."

"What are the other puppies named?" asked Dr. Emily. She was examining the biggest puppy, a male with a red ribbon, checking his teeth to make sure he had a proper bite. He was being as good as gold, as if he'd been through it all before.

"That's Berkeley," said Sara. "James has the other girl, Verona. And this one," she said, nodding toward the puppy whose ribbon was blue, "is Alfalfa. Alfie for short."

Alfie was climbing onto his mother's back with the determination of a mountaineer. Suddenly, he lost his balance and slid down Shan's shoulder to land flat on his back with his legs sticking up in the air. He stared up at Mandy, blinking in surprise.

"Oh, dear!" Mandy chuckled.

Alfie wriggled until he finally rolled over. He stood up and let out a high-pitched, indignant *Yip!*

Everyone laughed. Even Shan seemed amused, her mouth open in a wide doggy grin.

"He's such a character," said Sara, scooping him up. She held him in her arms as if he were a real baby, but he wriggled until she put him down again. "And he's the most adventurous," she added when he pounced on Dr. Emily's bag. "No, Alfie," she scolded, picking him up again. "That's not yours." He squirmed, wanting to be put down. As soon as his paws touched the ground, he leaped onto Sara's sneakers and tugged at the laces.

"I'll miss them all when they go to their new homes." Sara sighed. "But I think I'll miss Alfie the most."

"At least your mom's going to make sure they go to perfect homes," said James.

"Yes, but that's as hard as applying for a new job," said Sara. "Isn't that what you said, Mom?"

Mrs. Grant nodded.

"But, in a way, it *is* a job. A very important one," Mandy said, and she smiled down at Tulip, who was asleep in her arms.

Two

Mandy's mom was backing the Land Rover out of the Grants' driveway when her phone rang. "Take that for me please, Mandy," she said when she saw the call was from Grandma Hope.

"What's up, Gran?" Mandy asked.

"Parkin!"

"As in spicy ginger cake?" Mandy said, and saw James's face light up.

"Yes. Traditional Yorkshire parkin," said Gran. "I've just taken three loaves out of the oven. One's for you and your mom and dad if you'd like to come in and get it."

19

"We'll be right there!"

Tom and Dorothy Hope lived in Lilac Cottage, on the other side of Welford from Animal Ark. When Mandy and her mom and James arrived, Grandpa was in the front yard, raking up leaves. Normally, he loved gardening. Today, he looked hot and bothered. Mandy soon realized why. As fast as Grandpa could rake up the crisp red and gold leaves, the wind scattered them around again.

"I give up!" he said when Mandy and James went over to him. He leaned on his rake, pushed his cap back off his forehead, and wiped his hand across his brow. "This wind's determined to beat me."

"We'll help you," said James.

"There's no point in three of us going in circles," said Grandpa. His face was red, like he'd been in the sun all day.

"We won't if we scoop up the leaves," said James. "Do you have any cardboard?"

Grandpa thought for a moment. "You'll find a couple of old boxes in the shed," he said.

James went to the shed in the backyard and returned with four rectangular pieces of cardboard that he'd torn off the boxes. He gave Mandy two. "We can use them to catch the leaves and carry them to the bonfire pile," he said.

For fifteen minutes, Mandy and James chased after the leaves that escaped Grandpa's rake. Trapping them between their cardboard sheets, they scraped them off the ground and deposited them on the growing pile. Once they had collected a large enough pile of leaves, they would burn them, making sure to keep the flames well away from any trees or plants in the yard, and then use the ash to fertilize the flower beds. Mandy loved the way that even fallen leaves could be recycled for the good of their backyard! They pushed the pile of leaves down each time to stop the leaves from being blown away again. Still, the wind kept stirring them up and whipping them away, making more work for Grandpa. Mandy decided that there was only one way to deal with that. "Why don't we just set fire to the leaves we've gathered so far?"

"It's too late in the day," said Grandpa. "We would have to sit up half the night waiting for it to go out. And in this wind . . ." He frowned as more leaves took off and scudded through the air to land on the lawn a few yards away. ". . . it would be crazy to light a fire. Just one strong gust could send it out of control."

"But at this rate there won't be a bonfire pile in the morning," Mandy pointed out, plucking a big red leaf out of the air as it floated past her. "More like a carpet of leaves."

"We could cover it," said James.

"That's what I was thinking," said Grandpa. "Wait here one minute." He went to the shed and brought back a big blue tarp.

Mandy and James helped him stretch it over the mound of leaves. They collected fallen branches and placed them around the edge to weigh the cover down. By the time the job was done, the sun had set.

"You've been a big help," said Grandpa. "Let's see if there's something for us to eat inside."

Gran and Mandy's mom not only had a big pot of tea waiting for Grandpa and mugs of hot chocolate for Mandy and James, but a plate of parkin slices, too.

"You certainly deserve it after all that hard work," said Gran, offering the plate to James.

Mandy had just finished her hot chocolate, and James was starting on his fourth slice of parkin when Grandpa went to get a can of dog food from the pantry.

"What's that for?" Mandy asked. Her grandparents didn't own a dog.

Grandpa was rifling through the cutlery drawer. He glanced at Mandy, his eyes twinkling.

The suspense was too much for Mandy. "Don't tell me you got a dog and you've been keeping it a secret!"

Grandpa took out a can opener. "All will be revealed," he promised mysteriously, spooning some food into a dish. He looked at James, who was polishing off the crumbs on his plate. "Still hungry?"

James blushed. "No."

"Then come outside with me, both of you," said Grandpa. "Someone else wants a snack."

"Who?" Mandy pleaded, but Grandpa didn't say another word.

Outside, it was pitch-black except for where a rectangle of light spilled onto the patio from the kitchen window. Grandpa put the food on the edge of the patio and beckoned to Mandy and James to follow him to a bench beneath the kitchen window. "We'll wait here where we won't disturb our little friend," he said.

Mandy tried to think who the mystery visitor could be. A stray cat that Grandpa was trying to befriend so he could take it to the animal shelter? She was trying to recall any unfamiliar cats she'd seen recently in Welford, when she heard rustling coming from the shrubs on the far side of the patio.

A dark shape emerged from a bush. It didn't look big enough to be a cat. Or even a rabbit. Then, as it moved into the light, Mandy finally recognized it: a round little creature with a pointy face, short legs, tiny paws with long toes, and silvery spines bristling from its back.

"It's a hedgehog!"

The little creature went right to the saucer of dog food. He ate hungrily and seemed oblivious to everything else. Even a strong gust of wind that shook the tree next to the patio and ripped off the remaining leaves did not disturb him. Caught in the wind, the leaves spiraled upward before floating to the ground. One landed on the hedgehog's head, and he looked up with a start. Mandy held her breath. She hoped the hedgehog wouldn't scoot off in fright before he had finished his meal. She watched the leaf slide off his head and onto the ground. The hedgehog shot a wary glance at it, sniffed it, and, to Mandy's relief, resumed eating.

"Does he come here every night?" whispered James.

"I think so," murmured Grandpa. "But I only noticed him last Friday. He was snuffling around, looking for slugs and caterpillars. I figured that since he's about to hibernate for the winter, he could use some extra food. So Gran and I stocked up on dog food. It's easier than groveling around for bugs!"

"Why dog food?" said James, his face scrunched up as if he thought it was the last thing a hedgehog would want to eat.

"Dog food's fine," Mandy told him. "Better than, say, bread and milk, or oatmeal, because a hedgehog's natural diet is insects and bugs."

"Of course!" said James. "I should have remembered. Hedgehogs are insectivores. So food that carnivores eat is probably closer than an herbivore's food."

Mandy looked around and saw Gran and her mom peering out of the kitchen window. Gran smiled and mouthed something, but Mandy couldn't make out what it was.

"She's trying to tell you what we call him," said Grandpa, his blue eyes twinkling.

"What?" Mandy asked.

"Thistle," he replied.

Mandy twisted around again and gave Gran a thumbs-up. Thistle was the perfect name for a cute and prickly hedgehog!

Mandy and James saw the puppies again two days later when Mrs. Grant invited them to dinner. They arrived early so that they could play with the four-legged family before dinner. The puppies had other ideas, though. They were curled up and sound asleep when the three friends looked in at them.

"They're building up their strength for the next round of rough and tumble," whispered Sara as they tiptoed away. "So prepare yourselves for the onslaught later!"

Dinner wasn't ready yet, so Sara decided to show

them a project she'd started that afternoon. "I'm making a scrapbook for each puppy," she said, leading them to the living room, where a low table was covered in photographs, sheets of paper, felt-tip pens, glue, and four scrapbooks.

"I'm calling them 'Books of Life,'" said Sara. "Because they'll contain everything about the puppies, like a record of their weight from day one to the day they leave, photographs, their medical records, and other things, like when they first opened their eyes, and when they ate their first solid meal."

James was listening with interest. "All their milestones, in other words?"

"Exactly," said Sara. "I'll make copies for the new owners but I want to keep the originals so that I'll always remember them."

"It's a great idea," Mandy said as she picked up one of the books. It was covered in gold foil paper with ALFIE written in bold black capitals on a white label in the center. Above it was a photograph of Alfalfa peeping out from behind a potted plant with one of the glossy green leaves in his mouth! "That sums him up," Mandy said with a chuckle. She opened the book. There wasn't much in it yet, just one picture on the first page. It was of Shan licking her newborn puppy. The caption below said: *Alfalfa Grant, five minutes old!*

It was dated just over six weeks earlier, with the time: 3:25 A.M.

"Three-thirty in the morning!" said James, his eyes wide. "Shan really picked her moment."

"That's what Dad said." Sara smiled.

The other books were at the same stage as Alfie's — each covered in foil, with a photo and name on the front, and the very first picture of the puppy on page one. "I work on them whenever I get the chance," said Sara, gathering up the loose photographs all over the table. "But there's just so much going on. Moving, starting at a new school, a Halloween party coming up, a costume to make, puppies to feed and play with, Shan to take care of and walk every day — It's hectic sometimes. But I'm not complaining," she added hastily. "I wouldn't change any of it."

"It's not like it'll be hectic forever," said James. "Soon the puppies will go to their new homes."

"Don't remind me," said Sara, but she smiled so that Mandy knew she was resigned to them leaving eventually. "By the way," Sara added while she put the photographs inside large envelopes and stacked the scrapbooks in a neat pile, "there's a family coming to see them later this evening — the Wilsons. They called just after you left, when the puppies had their injections."

"The same day we met Thistle," Mandy recalled.

"Thistle?" said Sara, tightening the caps on the felt-tip pens.

"Yep. Thistle the hedgehog who eats like a dog." James chuckled. He picked up a pen from the floor.

Sara frowned. "What are you talking about?"

Mandy filled her in on Grandma and Grandpa Hope's nighttime visitor.

"It must have been great to see him," said Sara when Mandy had finished. "I wish I could get one to visit us. Maybe I should put out some of Shan's food."

James raised his eyebrows. "With a Labrador around?" He shook his head. "You don't stand a chance. If Shan's anything like Blackie when it comes to sniffing out food, a hedgehog wouldn't get a single bite."

"Who wouldn't get a single bite?" asked Mr. Grant, who was coming in just then. He had light brown hair, hazel eyes like Sara's, and was still in his formal work clothes — a dark suit, white shirt, and navy blue tie.

"The hedgehog," said Sara.

"What hedgehog?" said Mr. Grant. "Don't tell me we have another mouth to feed." He looked serious, but when Mandy saw him wink at James, she knew he was only teasing.

"I wish there was." Sara chuckled and told him about Thistle.

"Now that's the kind of animal I'd welcome, too," said Mr. Grant. "One that sleeps for nearly half the year! Speaking of food, dinner's on the table, folks."

An autumn feast of baked potatoes, sizzling sausages, and baked beans awaited them in the dining room.

"Yum," said James. "Spuds and sausages! My favorite."

Mrs. Grant put a bowl of grated cheese on the table. "Actually, they're veggie sausages, not meat ones, because we're vegetarians."

"I am, too!" Mandy said.

"*All* sausages are my favorite," James assured them.

They'd just finished doing the dishes after dinner when Mr. and Mrs. Wilson and their son, Rick, arrived. Rick was thirteen, with black hair and brown eyes, and he was almost as tall as his dad.

"We only recently moved to Walton," said Mrs. Wilson after everyone had been introduced. She was the shortest member of the family, slightly plump with a very round face. "We bought a vegetable farm not far from here. We promised Rick that once he settled in to his new school in York, and I'd settled in there, too — I teach math — we'd think about getting a puppy."

"I bet you didn't waste any time getting settled, Rick," Mandy said with a smile.

"Not a minute." He grinned. "I can't wait to see the puppies playing so I can get an idea of their personalities."

"What sort of dog are you looking for?" Mandy asked.

"A confident, sociable one," said Rick. "That's the right temperament for a Labrador. It means they're playful and love having fun, which is what I want to do!"

Mandy exchanged a glance with James. Rick seemed to know a lot about dogs.

"Have you had a dog before?" James asked as they went through to the puppy nursery.

"Never," Rick admitted. "But I've done plenty of research, especially on Labradors, and I really like playing with my uncle's sheepdogs on his farm in Northumberland. One of them had six puppies in the summer so I learned a lot about how to look after them."

Mandy crossed her fingers. Rick seemed like the perfect owner for one of Shan's babies.

Energized after their nap, the puppies were like jumping beans. Mandy had brought them a rope toy. She held it out, making it wriggle, then threw it across the floor. The puppies chased after it. Alfie got to it first. Clenching it in his teeth, he trotted back to Mandy.

"He's already a good retriever," she commented.

"He's great," Rick agreed. "But this one's terrific, too," he added when Berkeley grabbed the rope from Alfie and raced across to Rick, dropping it at his feet. He crouched down to pat Berkeley, who put up a soft little paw and batted Rick's hand. "Hey! You know how to give a high five, too."

Rick's parents glanced at each other, and Mr. Wilson put his hand on Rick's shoulder. "He is a good-looking puppy," he said, "and this is definitely the best litter we've seen so far. But I don't want you getting your hopes up too high, son. Like we told you earlier, with the cost of moving, we might not be able to afford an expensive breed right now."

Clearly disappointed, Rick gave his mom a pleading look. Mrs. Wilson sighed. "Dad's right. We've got to think about money. But we'll discuss it again at home."

Rick wanted to spend more time with the puppies so his parents agreed to stay for a while longer. He rolled a ball for them, and tossed the rope toy, and watched each puppy's reactions closely. It seemed to Mandy as if he was making an in-depth study of the litter. When it was time to leave, Rick gave each puppy one last cuddle, saving the biggest hug for Berkeley. "I hope I see you again soon, little guy," he said.

Mandy agreed silently, while Sara said, "Me, too!"

The front door had hardly closed behind the Wilsons when Sara started pleading with her mom to let Rick have the puppy at a lower price. "He wants one so badly and I just know he'd look after him really well."

Outside, the Wilsons' car started up. Through the hall window, Mandy glimpsed them driving away, Rick looking out of the back window as if to get a last look at Berkeley.

"I'm sure he would be a perfect owner," said Mrs. Grant as they went back to the puppies. "But I can't lower the price."

"You can," Sara insisted. "You always said we didn't want to make money off the puppies."

"And we won't make any, even at the full price," said her mom, shaking out the puppies' blanket. "It barely covers the cost of registering and raising the pups for the first couple of months. And, anyway," she added, putting the blanket back in the box, "there are other families who can offer just as good a home."

Mandy knew Mrs. Grant was right. Who wouldn't be willing to pay a good price for one of these gorgeous little dogs?

Three

"It's an avalanche of leaves!" Mandy exclaimed.

It was the following Saturday afternoon. Mandy was helping her parents rake leaves in their backyard.

"You'd never think so few trees could produce so many," said Dr. Adam, scooping handfuls of yellow leaves out of the birdbath.

Emily Hope was sweeping more off the front steps into an overflowing cardboard box. "Empty this out, please, Mandy," she said.

Mandy carried the box to the bonfire pile in the backyard lawn. The pile was so high, she had to stand on her toes to dump out the box. Returning to her mom, she said, "If the pile gets any higher, we'll have a mountain."

"And if the wind gets stronger, we'll have that avalanche you mentioned," said Dr. Emily.

Mandy was emptying out another load when James and Blackie arrived. "Just in time to join the leaf-clearing team," she said.

"Great," muttered James, unclipping Blackie's leash. "That's exactly why I came over this afternoon."

"To give us a hand?" Mandy asked.

"No. To get out of raking *our* backyard." But James didn't really mind helping and he was soon hard at work shoving leaves into a bag.

It was late in the afternoon when they'd finished. James surveyed the front yard. The lawn was empty, and the trees looked starkly bare without a carpet of leaves around their trunks. "Where's Blackie?" he said.

Mandy looked to where she'd last seen him sitting on the front doormat. He wasn't there now. "He probably got bored and went exploring," she said.

"Blackie!" called James.

Nothing.

"That's weird," said James. "Why isn't he coming?"

Mandy chuckled. "He doesn't normally."

"He does," said James as they went around to the

backyard. "He's good most of the —" He broke off. "Blackie! You bad, bad dog!"

Mandy groaned. "Oh, no!" Blackie was having the time of his life in the leaves that she and James had worked so hard to gather! He had pounced on the unlit bonfire pile, flattening it completely, and now he was whirling around like a windup toy, scattering leaves everywhere.

Mandy's parents came around the side of the house. "Oh, Blackie." Dr. Adam sighed. "You really are too much."

James's face was very red. "No more treats for you!" he said, marching over to Blackie.

The Labrador stopped mid-spin. Standing knee-deep in leaves, with his tongue hanging out at the side of his mouth, he looked as if he was laughing with glee.

Mandy had to stifle a laugh herself when James reached for Blackie's collar and grasped nothing but fresh air as Blackie sprang to one side.

"It's not a game," said James very sternly.

Blackie must have realized the fun was over. He sat down, flattened his ears low, and blinked at James. If he could talk, Mandy knew he'd be saying he was sorry.

James could read his dog like a book. "I don't care how sorry you are, so you can get rid of that hangdog expression." He reached for Blackie again. This time, Blackie kept still and James got ahold of his collar. "I'm locking you in the kitchen." He led the dog to the back door and pushed him inside, shutting the door firmly behind him.

It took Mandy and James half an hour to rebuild the bonfire pile. When it was heaped up again and ready to be lit, Dr. Adam attached a hose to the outside faucet. "Just in case we need to put it out," he said.

Dr. Emily had gone in to get refreshments. She came out with four mugs of steaming tomato soup. "Blackie's looking very sorry for himself," she said, handing the tray around.

"He should be," said James.

Mandy's dad struck a match and held it at the bottom of the pile. "Stand back, everyone."

The thinnest trail of smoke wafted out from beneath a leaf. It looked like it might fizzle out, but suddenly a small flame broke out. Within seconds, tongues of fire devoured the leaves, crackling and hissing.

The leaves were so dry, the fire burned out in the time it took for them to finish their soup. Within minutes, only a smoldering pile of ashes remained.

"Great teamwork," said Dr. Adam. "Thanks, all of you." He picked up the hose and went to turn on the faucet.

"No thanks to Blackie," said James.

"I think we can forgive him." Dr. Emily smiled. "He really didn't do any harm."

"He probably thought we piled the leaves up just for him," Mandy said.

James shrugged. "It's just really irritating to work so hard and find you have to do it all over again."

Dr. Adam aimed the hose at the ashes to dampen them. "I don't know about that. I think Blackie did you a favor."

James looked at him in surprise.

"I'm serious," said Dr. Adam, turning off the faucet.

"Think of all the extra exercise you got. It definitely qualifies you for a slice of Grandma's parkin. What do you say to that?"

"Yes, please!" said James.

In the kitchen, Blackie was lying under the table making snuffling noises.

James's eyes grew wide. "What are you up to now?" he said. He stormed to the table and bent down. Mandy heard him gasp before he cried out, "Oh, no!" Then, "You're impossible!"

"What did he do?" Mandy said. Kneeling next to James, she saw a cake container by Blackie's front paws. It was the same one Gran's parkin had been in.

But there was no parkin in it now.

"Oh, Blackie," Mandy said, "you're the greediest dog on earth."

Blackie must have thought Mandy was praising him. He thumped his tail on the floor.

"You mean he got into the cake?" said Dr. Adam, looking aghast.

James straightened up, his face bright red with embarrassment. "I'm really sorry. I shouldn't have left him in the kitchen."

"It's not your fault," said Dr. Emily.

"It is," James insisted. "I should have put him in the shed."

Dr. Emily shook her head. "No. It's my fault for leaving the container on the table. Blackie must have jumped up and knocked it off."

James looked even more embarrassed. "I hope he didn't scratch the table or eat anything else."

Dr. Adam was hanging his jacket behind the door. "I think we can safely say that Blackie has had his cake and eaten it."

"He probably even understood when you said there would be no more treats for him." Mandy chuckled. "So he found his own."

But James wasn't listening to any excuses for his dog. He clipped the leash onto his collar. "You've caused enough trouble for one day. We're going home." And he marched Blackie through the door.

Mandy watched them through the window until they disappeared down the road. "I bet James will forgive him before they get home," she said. Blackie was so good-natured, it was impossible to be angry with him for long.

Tired after the double dose of leaf gathering, Mandy got the latest copy of her favorite magazine, *Animal Parade*, which had arrived that morning. Curling up on the sofa, she looked at the photograph on the cover. It showed a young girl holding a tiny chestnut pony in her arms. WENDY MARKS AND HER BRAND-NEW FALABELLA PONY, TINA, read the caption.

"That's the sweetest pony ever." Mandy sighed. "And so cuddly." Not for the first time, she wished she had a pet of her own, one that would be curled up with her on the sofa at that very moment. She imagined what it would be like to come home to her own dog, or cat, or a miniature pony like Tina. But that would have to remain a dream. Mandy and her parents were too busy looking after other people's animals to have time for any of their own. It was a life that she wouldn't change for anything, though. *I get to make friends with new animals all the time*, she consoled herself.

She opened the magazine and scanned the list of contents. One item caught her eye: PROTECTING OUR THREATENED WILDLIFE. PART 2: RED SQUIRRELS. Mandy was as devoted to wildlife as she was to domestic animals. She turned to the article and was just getting into it when the phone rang.

She went to answer it. "Animal Ark," she said, but before she could give her name, the voice at the other end blurted out, "The puppies!"

"What about them?" Mandy said, recognizing Sara's voice.

"They're gone!" said Sara.

Four

"Gone?" Mandy echoed in dismay.

"Yes. This afternoon." Sara's voice was hoarse. "We went shopping for new carpets. When we came home, the back door was open and . . ." She broke off, gulped, then said in a rush, ". . . the puppies were gone! Stolen."

"No!" Mandy felt the blood drain from her face. "But . . . but . . ." Then she thought about the puppies' mother. "Where's Shan?"

"She was locked in the downstairs bathroom," said Sara. "We heard her scratching at the door and whining. And now . . ." She trailed off, sobbing.

Mandy found herself holding back tears as she waited for Sara to continue.

"She's . . . she's beside herself." Sara wept. "She's hunting everywhere for her babies."

"Poor, poor Shan." Unable to hold back her tears any longer, Mandy felt them rolling down her cheeks as she imagined the beautiful dog pacing back and forth, desperate to find her puppies. "Didn't the neighbors see anything suspicious?"

"We asked everyone on our street," said Sara. "No one saw any strangers or anything unusual."

"Someone's playing a Halloween trick," Mandy said. But she was grasping at straws. Who in their right mind would play such a cruel joke?

"Halloween's not for weeks. And no one would steal puppies for the fun of it. I mean, they're not even seven weeks old yet," said Sara, sobbing so much it was hard to hear her correctly. She paused as if to compose herself. "I don't know what we're going to do," she went on. "Do you think you and your parents could come over?"

Mandy wanted to help more than anything, but she couldn't think how they could be of any real use right then. "What about the police?" she said.

"Mom's already phoned them. They're on their way," said Sara. "But I wish you'd come, too. Shan's so upset.

I was hoping your mom and dad could do something for her."

Mandy imagined a human mother in a similar situation. A doctor would be called in to give her something to help her over the shock. Just because Shan was a dog didn't mean she wouldn't be just as desperate. "I'll talk to my dad," she promised.

She found him coming out of the residential unit after checking on the only patient there: Herman, a small crossbreed dog. He was another victim of the strong wind, hurt when a branch fell onto his back.

"Is he still hurting a lot?" Mandy asked.

"Not too badly. I gave him a painkiller and a light sedative," said her dad. "But what's up with you? You look like the world's on your shoulders."

"The most terrible thing has happened!" Mandy burst out. She told him about the missing puppies. "Sara wants us to come over, but I don't know if there's anything we can do," she finished.

"Actually, there is," said Dr. Adam, going to his treatment room. "I know the puppies are nearly weaned and are on four meals a day, but they're probably still nursing when they get the chance. If they're not there to drink Shan's milk, she could develop mastitis."

"Mastitis?"

Dr. Adam opened the medicine cabinet. "It's a painful infection that nursing animals can develop. Shan will need an injection to stop her from making more milk."

It seemed such a drastic step, and it suggested to Mandy that her dad didn't have much hope of the puppies coming back soon.

On the way to the Grants' house, Mandy and her dad picked up James. Mandy had called to tell him the terrible news. He'd only just gotten home from Animal Ark with Blackie when Mandy phoned, but he was ready to leave again right away. "We've got to find them!" he vowed.

They found Sara sitting on the kitchen floor, hugging Shan. Tears streamed down her cheeks, and the more she tried to wipe them away, the more they flowed. Shan looked utterly miserable, too. No longer the proud, happy dog she'd been just yesterday, she held her head low and stared at the ground with dull eyes. Even when Mandy crouched next to her, Shan barely looked at her.

"If only you could talk," Mandy said, stroking her. "You might be able to tell us who the thief was."

"She tried," said Sara. "She sniffed around the back door and picked up a trail. She followed it around to the front yard but lost it by the gate."

"Which suggests the thief might have driven away at that point," said James. He wrote something in a notebook, then looked through the utility room to the back door, where two policemen were taking fingerprints. "Let's hope they get some clear ones," he said. "In the meantime, we have to write down every clue, even if it doesn't seem important."

Mr. and Mrs. Grant and a policewoman were in the backyard, looking across the field in the direction of the woods.

"A possible escape route," said James, making another note.

"The woods?" Mandy asked.

"Yep. Dense cover and lots of places to hide," said James.

"A policeman's already searching them," said Sara. She sniffed and wiped her cheeks with her hand. "But the thief's probably miles away already."

Mandy saw the policewoman say something to Sara's parents, then she went out the back gate and headed into the woods. Mr. and Mrs. Grant came inside, their faces pinched with worry.

"We shouldn't have left the puppies and Shan on their own," Mr. Grant said grimly.

"You can't blame yourselves," said Dr. Adam. "It's impossible to keep an eye on puppies every hour of the day. And it's not as if you were careless. They were locked in the house when you went out, weren't they?"

Mrs. Grant nodded.

Dr. Adam took a syringe out of his bag. "Has anyone been snooping around lately?" he asked, peeling away the sterile plastic packaging.

James lifted his pen, ready to note down new clues.

"Not that we can remember," said Mrs. Grant.

"The culprit could be any of dozens of people," said

Mr. Grant. "Since we moved in, there's been a steady stream of visitors: decorators, movers, and people coming to see the pups."

James was scribbling in his notebook as fast as Mr. Grant was speaking. Mandy looked over his shoulder. There was a heading on the page: *Prime Suspects*. Beneath it was a list.

1. *People coming to see the pups — get details and check on those we can trace.*
2. *Decorators — get phone numbers, addresses.*
3. *Furniture moving company — telephone number? Ask them to check if the pups got inside the vans (could they have climbed into a van???)*
4. *Pet shops? Shady ones? Check them out.*

James, it seemed, was determined to leave no stone unturned.

Mrs. Grant picked up the *Walton Gazette*. "There's also the ad in here," she said, flicking through the pages until she came to it. "Lots of people must have seen it. I even stated that the pups were very well bred." She sighed. "That would have been like honey to a bee. What dog thief could resist? And if that wasn't enough . . ." She jabbed the page with her forefinger. "I gave our address." She flung the paper aside. "To think I could have been so stupid! It was an open invitation to thieves."

Dr. Adam took a small glass vial out of his bag. He snapped off the top, which he passed to Mandy to throw away, and drew Shan's medication into the syringe. "But you had to advertise the puppies," he said, "and naturally, people would want to know their pedigree and where to come to see them." He knelt next to Shan and gently inserted the needle into her shoulder. The dog didn't even flinch. It was like she'd blocked out everything except the pain of losing her puppies.

Mandy crouched next to her again. She waited for her dad to withdraw the needle, then she gently rubbed the spot where it had gone in. She looked across Shan's back and caught Sara's eye.

"She's been the best mother ever," Sara whispered. "She doesn't deserve any of this." She hugged Shan. "She must think she's being punished even though she's done nothing wrong."

James was still taking notes. He flipped the page over and kept writing.

Dr. Adam closed his bag. "I think we've done all we can, Mandy," he said quietly. "We'll head home now." He must have seen her reluctance because he added, "We don't want to get in anyone's way."

On the drive back to Welford, no one had the heart
to say anything. Mandy and her dad and James just
stared out the windows, their silence underlining their
sadness.

Mandy's thoughts drifted from Shan to the puppies to
Shan again and back to the puppies. Where could they be
at that very moment? Were they safe, warm, and loved?
Or were they in some horrible cage being transported
to a distant place? Maybe they'd been left outdoors
where they were being buffeted by the cold wind while
they waited for whatever fate had in store for them.

Wherever the puppies were, Mandy decided that
only the most callous person could have taken them
from their mother and locked her up so she couldn't
go after them.

It was dark when Dr. Adam drove in through the gate
at Animal Ark. With her mind so full of the puppies, Mandy only noticed the figure crossing the lawn
when she jumped down from the Land Rover.
"It's Grandpa!" she said, and went across to him. "Hi,
Grandpa. Is everything okay?"

"Fine," he said. "Except that we've run out of dog
food for Thistle. By the time I realized, the store was
already closed. So I came over to borrow some."

Dr. Adam opened the front door and they all went
inside. "Who's Thistle?" he asked.

"No one told you?" said Grandpa, wiping his shoes on the mat.

"Nope," said Dr. Adam, switching on the hall light.

Grandpa looked surprised. "I thought half the world would have heard by now. Thistle's our little hedge . . . er . . ." He grinned at Mandy. ". . . dog."

Any other time, Mandy would have laughed. Now, though, she was too gloomy to even smile.

At first, Grandpa didn't seem to notice. He was reaching into his pocket, saying, "Take a look at these pictures. I took them last night with my new digital camera and printed them myself. Aren't they great?" He handed half to Mandy and the rest to James.

"They're okay," said James, while Mandy simply glanced at them before passing them to her dad.

"Cute hedgehog," was all Dr. Adam said before he gave the photographs back to Grandpa.

"Oh, well . . . if that's how it is," said Grandpa. Clearly, he was miffed that no one seemed interested in his pictures. He put them back in his pocket and said, "What's wrong with you all? You're as miserable as the weather."

"Sorry, Grandpa," Mandy said. "But something horrible has happened." She explained about the puppies.

Grandpa went pale. "I can't believe anyone could do

such a thing!" he said, following Dr. Adam into the living room. "What is this world coming to?"

"James and I are going over tomorrow to help track down the thief," Mandy told him.

"Good, good," murmured Grandpa. "The poor little things will be so frightened." He turned to go out, passing Dr. Emily, who looked perplexed when he said, "I must tell Gran. She could spread the word among her friends." Seconds later, the front door slammed behind him.

Mandy realized he hadn't taken any dog food with him. She ran to the storeroom and got two cans, then called to him out of the window. "Wait, Grandpa!" But he was already at the gate and didn't hear her.

"I'll go after him," said James. Grabbing the cans from Mandy, he raced outside, calling, "You forgot Thistle's dog food!"

Mandy watched James disappear down the road.

Next to her, Dr. Adam said, "That's one lucky hedgehog."

Mandy nodded. But as she stared into the darkness, she could think only of the puppies and how desperate they must be for their mother.

Five

Dr. Emily gave Mandy and James a lift to the Grants'
house the next morning. They took their bikes, putting
them on the rack at the back of the Land Rover, so that
they'd be ready for a puppy-seeking expedition.

Sara met them at the front door. Her eyes were puffy,
as if she'd cried herself to sleep the night before. "No
news, except that there were two sets of fingerprints,"
she said, taking Mandy and James around to the backyard, where they leaned their bikes against a stack of
unopened bags of topsoil. "But the police haven't found
any matches, and not a single other clue." She looked to
where her parents and two policemen were coming out

of the shed. "They checked to see if anything else was stolen, in case it was an ordinary burglary and the puppies got out by themselves when the door was left open."

"And?" James prompted, opening his notebook.

Sara shook her head. "Nothing else is missing. And we know that Shan couldn't have shut herself in the bathroom."

"How can you tell?" Mandy asked.

"The door catches on the carpet and you have to give it a shove to shut it behind you," Sara explained.

They went in through the back door, squeezing past a man who was repairing the damage the thieves caused. "Mom said it was lucky we found someone to come out on a Sunday," said Sara on the way through the utility room. The sight of the puppies' empty bed made Mandy bite her lip.

Shan was in the kitchen. She gazed up at Mandy, her eyes filled with sad longing. Even though she was well loved, she looked like the loneliest dog on earth.

Mandy felt as if her heart would break. She put her arms around Shan. "We'll search everywhere," she whispered, but she stopped short of promising that they'd find the puppies. They'd been missing for nearly a day; they could be anywhere by now.

Sitting around the kitchen table, the three friends planned their next move.

"We need to figure out our strategy first," said James. He turned to a fresh page in his notebook. "I've made a list of suspects. We'll interview them or tail them, until we find our man. . . . I mean, the culprits. We can't rule out *anyone*."

"No, but we also can't suspect *everyone*," Mandy said.

"Just because someone's been here doesn't automatically make them a suspect," said Sara.

James gave the carpenter a furtive glance. "A thief will often return to the scene of the crime," he whispered.

Mandy rolled her eyes. "That's stupid. He's here for a real reason," she said under her breath. It was all very well to leave no stone unturned, but putting two and two together to make twenty-two was nutty!

"I guess," said James, sounding unconvinced.

Mandy suggested a well-known pet dealer in York who advertised he could get any breed of dog people wanted. "It makes you wonder where he actually gets them," she said as James jotted down the name.

Sara thought they should check out the garbagemen and the milkman. "I'm not saying they're suspects," she said, "but they could have seen something."

When the list was complete, James showed it to Mandy and Sara.

"Rick Wilson!" said Sara when she saw the name at the top. "You can't be serious. He was crazy about the puppies."

James was biting the end of his pen. "And that's exactly why he's suspect number one," he said. "He wanted a puppy so much but his dad said they might not be able to afford one. Rick was really disappointed — enough to want to steal them."

Sara's eyes stretched wide. "You could be right," she said, and even Mandy had to admit that James had a point.

"So, what are we waiting for?" he said. "I know where they live — Rick told me. Let's ride over and take a look around."

Mrs. Grant had come in toward the end of the conversation. She put up both hands and said, "Whoa! You can't accuse people of theft on the basis of very flimsy evidence."

James pulled on his jacket. "We won't accuse anyone," he said, sliding his pen and the notebook into his top pocket. "We'll just scout around, looking for clues."

"As long as that's all," said Mrs. Grant. She took some tomatoes out of the vegetable basket. "Lunch will be ready in an hour. If you see anything suspicious, come straight back and tell us. Don't take the law into your own hands."

The Wilsons' farm was a few miles down the road that ran north from Walton. It was only when they were approaching it that Mandy realized it was on the other side of the woods behind the Grants' house. "If it was Rick who took the puppies, he could have been home in no time," Mandy said.

They stopped at the side of the road. Straddling their bikes, they stared at the neat stone house fifty yards away. The wind tugged at their clothes and whipped their hair across their faces.

"There must be a lot of places on a farm to hide puppies," said James, pushing his hair off his forehead.

"So what do we do now? Knock on the door, tell Rick the puppies have been stolen, and ask him if he's heard anything?" said Sara, pulling up the hood of her parka. "Or hide our bikes, cut through that pumpkin field . . ." She pointed to the far side of the farmhouse. Bright orange pumpkins, ready for Halloween, dotted the field, interrupting the greenness of the vines they sat among. ". . . and check out the farm to see if the puppies are in a barn or something?"

Before they could decide on their next move, Rick appeared on the doorstep. He jogged down the path and through the gate. "I thought I recognized you," he said, coming closer.

"Hi, Rick," Mandy said, hoping her smile looked genuine and that her voice sounded natural. "We were just, er . . ."

"Seeing if you were home," Sara put in quickly. She looked cold, her eyes watering from the icy wind. She zipped up her parka and drew the string of the hood tighter. A few blond strands of hair escaped and blew into her eyes. "You're such a dog fan," she added, wiping the hair out of her eyes, "we wanted to keep in touch with you."

"Oh, yeah?" responded Rick. He came right up to them and stood with his arms folded.

"Yeah, we're crazy about dogs, too," said James, and Mandy saw him push the notebook down farther in his pocket.

"Then you should be telling me about the puppies," said Rick, his tone icy like the wind.

Mandy suddenly felt awkward. "The thing is . . . they've been —"

"Stolen," Rick butted in. "I heard about that." He narrowed his eyes. "I bet you think I took them, don't you? And you came to spy on me."

"It's not like that," Mandy protested.

"It is," said Rick. "Otherwise you'd have come right out with the news instead of pretending to be friendly."

Mandy didn't know what to say. Rick had caught them off guard.

James was inspecting his handlebars like there was a huge but invisible problem with them, while Sara started chewing the inside of her cheek. Mandy felt a drop of rain on her nose. She turned her face up to the sky. A steady drizzle dampened her cheeks and forehead and trickled down her neck. A storm was on the way.

It was Rick who broke the silence. "You're a hundred percent right."

With a gasp, Mandy looked at him. She heard Sara breathe in sharply and James exclaim, "I knew it!"

"I *am* a dog fan," Rick continued, "so I'd *never* do something like that." His brown eyes flashed with anger. Narrowing them, he stared at James. "I can't believe you could even *think* I would."

James grimaced. "I'm really sorry," he said, his face red. "It was my idea."

"And mine," said Sara hastily.

"We have to rule out everyone who's had any contact with the puppies," continued James.

Mandy nodded. "We can't leave any stone unturned," she muttered, but as she looked past Rick to the storage sheds and barns in the farmyard, she wondered if he wasn't just trying to make them leave quickly. What if the puppies were hidden close by after all and Rick was worried they'd make a noise that would give him away?

She heard him cough and when she looked back at him, she saw he was staring at her. He jabbed his thumb toward the house. "You can search the whole farm if you like." He must have guessed what was going

through Mandy's mind! "You'll see for yourselves that I don't have the puppies." But his expression suddenly softened. "Look, I'm really upset about them, too. I hate to think of them being scared and looking everywhere for Shan. So I'll keep my eyes open for anything suspicious."

"Thank you," called Sara as Rick walked back to the house. "We'll let you know if we come up with anything."

James kicked the ground in embarrassment while Sara stared after Rick, chewing her nails. Mandy squirmed inside. If only they'd been up front from the start, they might have had a friend on their side instead of making Rick think they didn't trust him.

The rain started falling harder, the wind blasting it into their faces. "That's that, then," said James.

They pedaled away, the storm buffeting them so that they were soon soaked through. All the way back to the Grants', no one said another word about their puppy-finding strategy. Mandy felt very gloomy. They were going to have to be careful not to make any more blunders like that.

At Sara's house, they peeled off their jackets and hung them to dry on the coatrack that stood next to the empty puppy box. When they went into the kitchen, Mrs. Grant was on the phone, telling one of her friends about the puppies.

It was only when they were all sitting down to lunch that Mr. Grant gave them a puzzled look. "Everyone's so solemn," he said. "I expected you'd come back full of news. Did you find out anything?"

"Not yet," said James.

"Except we're pretty certain that the thief wasn't Rick," said Sara, pushing her food around her plate as if she had no appetite.

"So we're no closer to finding the culprits," Mandy said.

James crossed something off the list in his notebook: Rick's name, Mandy realized. "We'll try another lead this afternoon," said James. "We could question the garbagemen."

But it was still raining after lunch so they couldn't go out after all.

"You could spend the time planning your Halloween costumes," said Mrs. Grant when she found them staring through the French doors in the living room. Shan was next to Mandy, gazing out sadly, too. "I found some library books that might give you some ideas," Mrs. Grant continued. She pointed to a pile of books on the coffee table. They were big and glossy, with titles like *Party Costumes* and *Halloween Outfits for All Events*. When no one showed any interest, Mrs. Grant put her arm around Sara. "I know your heart's broken, dearest. But life goes on. And it doesn't mean we have to give up hope."

"I guess," said Sara. Going over to the table, she picked up *Party Costumes.*

Hard as they tried, none of them could work up much excitement about their outfits or the party. Sara soon tossed aside *Party Costumes* in favor of the puppies' scrapbooks. She hadn't made much more progress but she stared at what she'd done so far, wiping away tears.

Mandy flicked halfheartedly through the costume books. She still hadn't decided what she was going to dress up as, but when she saw a skeleton, she thought it seemed like a cute idea. "I just have to paint bones onto a long-sleeved black T-shirt and black leggings," she said.

"There are stencils for the different bones," James pointed out, looking over her shoulder. "You could trace them and outline them on the clothes."

Sara offered to get some tracing paper and a pencil. Sitting on the floor in front of the coffee table, with Shan's head on her lap, Mandy traced the bones' shapes. So that she'd know where they fit in when it came to painting them onto the clothes, she labeled each drawing, copying the names given in the book — names like clavicle, scapula, radius, humerus, and tarsal.

"Phalanges?" James said, looking over her shoulder as she labeled the drawing she'd just finished.

"It's the scientific name for fingers and toes," Mandy said.

"Fingers and toes will do," said James. He showed her a picture of a pirate costume he'd found. "What do you think of this?"

Mandy wrinkled her nose. "I can't see myself as a pirate."

"Not you. Me," said James.

"I thought you'd nearly finished your jack-o'-lantern costume," said Sara, glancing up from a photo of Alfie climbing into the laundry basket.

James shrugged. "I've changed my mind. Dad said I looked like a big lampshade."

"That's what Susan Collins thought," said Mandy.

"Really? I could end up being the laughingstock of the school," said James. "James and the Giant Lampshade. It sounds like a bad movie." He looked so glum that Mandy couldn't help chuckling.

It was the only lighthearted moment of the day so far and Mandy hoped it might help to cheer Sara up. It didn't, though, and when Mandy saw Sara put aside the puppies' Books of Life and start looking through a pile of photographs, she noticed she was crying again, her tears flowing silently down her face.

*   *   *

"Besides the fingerprints, there's not a single clue," Mandy told her mom on the way home.

"So the trail's gone cold?" Dr. Emily asked, turning onto James's driveway.

"Only for now," said James. "Mandy and I are having a brainstorming session later. The thieves must have left some clues. We just have to know where to look."

Blackie was waiting for them in the hall. Having been shut up all day, he was so excited to see Mandy and James that he leaped up and almost knocked them both back out onto the porch.

"Cool it, Blackie," said James, pushing him down.

Blackie jumped up again, wagging his tail so fast, it was a blur of black.

James pushed him down again and headed for the kitchen. But Blackie barged ahead. He was back in a flash, carrying his leash in his mouth.

"He's trying to tell you something." Mandy chuckled.

James smiled. "He might be a little crazy sometimes, but he's brainy, too."

"Enough to have you wrapped around his little . . . er . . . phalange," Mandy said.

There was just enough daylight left for them to take Blackie to a nearby field. The rain had stopped, but the wind was as strong as ever. Full of pent-up energy,

Blackie dragged James all the way to the field. "It's like trying to hold back a train," he said, leaning backward until the leash was as taut as a steel cable.

At the field, James tried to unclip the leash. Blackie bounced up and down impatiently, making it hard for James to get ahold of the clasp. "Wait, will you?" he said.

Amused, Mandy stood in front of Blackie and said in a very stern voice, "Sit!"

He obeyed immediately.

"Sheesh," muttered James, shooting Mandy a look of respect. "I'd sit, too, if someone spoke to me like that." He released Blackie, who tore over to a chestnut tree in the middle of the field. The tree was bare, its leaves a golden-red carpet covering the ground.

For Blackie, though, they meant a heap of fun. He dived into them, sending them shooting into the air like a fountain. As they all rained back down on him, he flopped onto the ground. Soon, he was covered in leaves, only his face poking out, and grinning like he'd landed in paradise.

"Something tells me," Mandy said, "that fall's his favorite season."

"Yep," said James. "He's a Labrador who really loves leaves!"

Six

Back at James's house, they kicked around lots of ideas during their crime-busting session. They thought about looking for footprints in the field behind the Grants' house, but realized the rain would probably have wiped any out. Mandy suggested scouring the house and the yard in case the thieves had dropped something, but James reminded her that the police had already done their own search and found nothing.

"A tracker dog might have been able to pick up a scent," Mandy said, just as her dad arrived to take her home. "Except the rain probably washed any scent away."

"If there ever was one," said James. "If the thieves

came by car, the trail would have stopped where they parked."

Mandy felt utterly dejected when she went to bed that night. The police hadn't made any progress, so how could they? The thieves had covered their tracks too well. It was as if the puppies had vanished into thin air.

She awoke the next morning to a bright, clear day. But when she called Sara and learned there was still no news, even the sunshine wasn't enough to lift her mood. It was the worst start to the midterm break anyone could imagine. And for Sara, it had to be like a waking nightmare. Mandy knew there wasn't much she could do to make her feel better, other than to offer her moral support.

When her dad dropped her at the Grants' house after breakfast, Mandy was shocked at how Sara looked. There were dark rings under her eyes, and she was as pale as ashes.

"I hardly slept last night," Sara confessed when she let Mandy in. Shan was at her side, looking very unhappy, too, even though Sara was holding her leash, ready to take her out for a walk. Shan greeted Mandy by nudging her hand with her wet nose, before staring sadly out the door as if she hoped to get a glimpse of her puppies.

"I just keep thinking of them and how they must be missing Shan," Sara continued, putting on her jacket.

"Me, too," Mandy said. "But we've got to believe that whoever stole them won't hurt them."

Sara clipped on the leash. "I wish I could believe that."

"Think about it," said Mandy as they went down the

driveway. A white van turned in through the gate. Mandy recognized the landscapers, Faye and Peter Cole, coming to work. She stood to one side with Sara and Shan and waved to them when they drove past.

"You were going to tell me why you believe the puppies are being looked after carefully," Sara reminded Mandy as they went on again.

"Well, if the people who stole them want them as pets, surely they'll take good care of them," Mandy said. There was another possibility, though. "But the thieves might have also taken them because they realize they're worth a lot of money. They could be planning to sell them to people who want to breed them."

Sara nodded. "And to get a good price for them, they'll have to make sure they're in good condition," she said, following Mandy's train of thought.

"Exactly. No one's going to want to pay a lot for a sick, miserable-looking puppy." It was a small consolation, but it was something to cling to.

In the park, Sara kept Shan on her leash in case she decided to run off to look for her puppies. Other people were out with their dogs, and when a family arrived with two young Staffordshire bull terrier puppies who raced up to Mandy and Sara then tumbled around at Shan's feet, it was more than Sara could bear. "Let's go," she said, turning away.

Back at Sara's house, they were sorting through the puppies' photographs — each one like a stab in the heart for Mandy — when Mrs. Grant came in. She was holding a letter. From the look on her face, it contained more bad news.

"What is it?" asked Sara.

Mrs. Grant sighed. "I can hardly believe this is happening."

Mandy saw the blood drain from Sara's already ashen face and felt a knot tighten in her stomach. *Don't let the puppies be hurt,* she prayed silently.

"This is from Mrs. Rawdon," said Mrs. Grant, waving the letter before her. "She owns Ennis."

"The puppies' father," said Sara.

"He's just been diagnosed with . . ." Mrs. Grant looked at the letter again. "*Progressive retinal atrophy,*" she read out loud.

"What's that?" said Sara while Mandy tried to recall if she'd ever heard of it.

"*PRA is a genetic condition,*" Mrs. Grant read, "*that affects a dog's eyesight.*"

"You mean Ennis could go blind?" Mandy hadn't heard of the disease before, and wished her parents were there to tell her more about it.

Mrs. Grant nodded without looking up. "Not could. *Will.* Apparently, he has central PRA. It's when the center field of sight is affected. It takes a few years to develop but over time, a dog sees less and less clearly."

"That's so sad," said Sara. "Can't the vet do anything?"

"Not much," said her mom. "Mrs. Rawdon says there's no cure. But it will be a long time before Ennis is completely blind."

Sara looked slightly relieved.

"At least he'll have a normal life for a few years," Mandy said.

"Oh, no," said Mrs. Grant, still studying the letter. "There's something else." She looked at Mandy and Sara again, her expression grim. Suddenly, the air seemed to turn icy, while the silence in the room grew heavier. On the mantelpiece, an old-fashioned clock ticked away the seconds.

At last, Mrs. Grant spoke again. "Because PRA is a genetic condition, Ennis cannot be allowed to sire any more puppies. And the ones he has already fathered mustn't be used for breeding, either."

For a moment, the full meaning of this didn't sink in, but as Mandy thought about it, everything became horribly clear. "Ennis could have passed PRA on to his puppies," she said, feeling sick to the core.

"You mean the puppies will go blind as well?" Sara gasped.

Mrs. Grant put the letter on the table. "The chances are very high that Ennis will have passed the deficient gene to them. They could go blind, and they could also pass the gene on to any puppies of their own."

It was a huge blow, a real double whammy, and for the rest of the morning, Mandy and Sara were in a slump of despair. All they could do was look at the pictures of the puppies over and over again. The photographs showed the four at every stage of their development so far, from the moment they were born with their little faces scrunched up and their eyes tightly closed. Pictures taken a day later showed them wearing the different colored ribbons that identified them. At ten days, Verona and Tulip had opened their eyes, and the photographs taken the following day showed Alfie and Berkeley seeing the world for the first time, too.

In other pictures, the puppies' curiosity was plain to see. There was one of them peering into the camera, frowning as they tried to figure out what the strange object was. Another showed Tulip sniffing at the broom she'd spotted in a corner, and there was one of Berkeley following a tiny black dot that Sara said was a beetle. In another photograph, Verona had pounced on a petal that had dropped off a flower in a vase. But for Mandy, the best picture of all was the one of Alfie skidding to a halt when he saw himself coming toward his own reflection in a mirror!

Almost every one of the pictures showed the puppies delighting in the world around them, checking out everything that caught their eye. *Everything that caught their eye.* How long, though, Mandy thought with a shiver, before their eyes started to fail, closing the fun-loving, curious puppies off from their world?

It was bad enough that they had been stolen, but to have a serious disease hovering over their future made everything a thousand times worse.

"I just can't believe it," Sara kept saying.

Although Mrs. Grant had told them a bit about PRA, there was still a lot they wanted to know, so when Dr. Adam arrived at lunchtime to get Mandy, he was met with a barrage of questions.

"Is it rare?" Sara asked. Mandy thought she knew what was behind Sara's question. If PRA was very unusual, the puppies might just be lucky enough not to have it.

Mrs. Grant poured out a cup of tea for Dr. Adam.

"Thank you," he said, and sat down at the kitchen table. "PRA is quite common," he began.

Sara groaned.

"Most vets will encounter several cases a year," Dr. Adam continued. "It's not uncommon in Labradors . . ." This made Sara look even more disheartened. ". . . but it occurs in every registered breed, and in mixed breeds. In some, like Irish setters, collies, and cairn terriers, it begins at a very early age so we can diagnose it when they're still young. In others, though, like miniature schnauzers and Labradors, the onset is much later. There's no reliable way of testing for it until the first signs appear."

Mrs. Grant sat down with her own cup of tea. "That would explain why Ennis's owner didn't know and she let him father the puppies," she said. "In her letter she said that he looked perfectly normal until a couple of weeks ago when she noticed his eyes seemed shiny."

"That's one of the first signs," said Dr. Adam. Shan had been lying on her mat in the corner. She got up, padded over to Dr. Adam, and rested her chin on his knee. He stroked her head. "And it's not just dogs that get it," he said, as if to comfort Shan. "Humans get it, too, but in us it's called retinitis pigmentosa."

"I knew someone who had retinitis pigmentosa," said Mrs. Grant. "A friend of my mother's. She was blind by the time she was sixty." She leaned back in her chair and rubbed her eyes as if she was tired. "I never imagined we'd confront it, too."

"Is there really nothing that can be done for Ennis?" Mandy pleaded.

"I'm afraid not," her dad said. "It's the retinal tissue inside the eye that dies. We can't stop that from happening. And although some people think that vitamin therapy can help to slow down the progress of the condition, studies haven't proven it." He finished his tea. "It's not all gloom, though. Ennis will lead a long and happy life, and because PRA develops very slowly in Labradors, he'll have a chance to adjust. His owner will be able to adjust as well, by learning how to make life easier for Ennis when he's completely blind."

"And by not using him for breeding again," said Mrs. Grant.

Dr. Adam nodded. "Yes, a lot of extra heartache could have been prevented." He didn't have to spell out what he meant; Mandy knew he was talking about the pain of knowing that four beloved puppies might go blind, and the sadness, too, of not being able to explain to the dog why his world was growing darker and fuzzier. And there was the more immediate anguish, the one most urgent of all, of knowing that the puppies were with people who knew nothing about their background.

Mrs. Grant stirred her tea. "This puts a new spin on the article that's appearing in the local paper tomorrow," she said. "I wonder if we should mention that the puppies could go blind. If the thieves find out, they might bring them back because they'll realize they aren't worth anything."

"You mean not worth any money," said Sara. "They're still the most precious puppies ever."

"Yes, of course," said Mrs. Grant.

Mandy thought it was a good idea to include the information.

But Sara saw things differently. "If these people stole the puppies in the first place, they're cruel enough to stop taking care of them if there's something wrong with them. They might even hurt them deliberately because they aren't worth anything now!"

"There's another possibility," said Dr. Adam. "The thieves might not think twice about lying. They could say nothing about PRA and simply pass the puppies off as being suitable for breeding." He took his cup over to the sink and rinsed it. "Not only would the new owners be cheated, but the gene could be spread further."

"Then we need to try harder to find them," Mandy said.

"Sara doesn't want her mom to tell the newspaper people about the PRA in case the thieves get angry and do something horrible to the puppies," Mandy told James later that afternoon. They were at Lilac Cottage with Dr. Adam to help Grandpa light the bonfire.

James was tying Blackie's leash to a wooden bench. When they had arrived a few minutes before, Blackie had made a beeline for the bonfire pile even though the tarp still covered it. James had dragged him away. The last thing they needed was another flattened pile of leaves. "How could anyone harm innocent puppies?" James said, taking a dog chew out of his pocket.

"I guess you can never tell," Mandy said.

James gave Blackie the chew, then he and Mandy helped Grandpa and Dr. Adam remove the branches weighing down the tarp. Each holding a corner, they lifted the sheet off the pile, being careful not to disturb the leaves.

Behind them, Blackie whined, disappointed at not being allowed to join in the fun.

"This is going to be some fire," said Dr. Adam. "It's twice the size ours was."

Blackie's whining became frantic barking. Mandy glanced back and saw him straining at his leash.

"Stop it, Blackie," said James. "You're not getting into these leaves."

Blackie ignored him. There was no letup to his barking and he bucked around, desperate to get free.

Grandpa laughed. "Who'd have thought a dog could be so crazy for leaves?"

"You should have seen him in our leaf pile." Mandy chuckled. "He was like a pig in clover!"

James frowned, his hands on his hips. "How dare you call my dog a pig?" he said, pretending to be outraged.

"There's nothing wrong with pigs," Mandy said. "They can be really sweet pets."

More leaves and twigs had blown down since the bonfire was built. Mandy and James gathered those up while Mandy's dad went to fetch a box of matches from the kitchen. By the time he joined the others again, Blackie's desperation had reached a fever pitch. His whining was like a siren and he was jumping up and down and lunging forward, trying to slip out of his collar.

"He's going to wear himself to a frazzle," Mandy said. Just then, everything went quiet. Looking around, she saw that Blackie's back legs were tangled in the leash. "You nutty dog! You've tied yourself up in knots." She tossed an armful of twigs onto the pile and turned to go and untangle Blackie, but James was already on his way over.

"Can't you keep still for a few minutes?" he asked, unclipping the leash. He gripped Blackie's collar while unwinding the leash with his free hand. Blackie saw his chance. With a jerk of his head, he wrenched himself out of James's grasp and hurtled toward the leaf pile, nearly careening into Dr. Adam, who was about to strike a match.

"Come back here, Blackie!" shouted James, charging after him.

Blackie hit the pile like a missile, landing in the center.

"Don't you dare. . . ." Mandy said, darting forward to haul him out before he could burrow into the leaves and send them swirling everywhere.

To her surprise, Blackie came to an abrupt stop. Standing stiff-legged, he stared down at his front paws with a rapt look on his face. The only part of him that moved was his tail, which was wagging a mile a minute.

Thinking Blackie was taking a breather before he got to work demolishing the pile, Mandy reached for his collar. It was only then that she saw what he was staring at: a prickly little mound between his front paws.

"It's Thistle!"

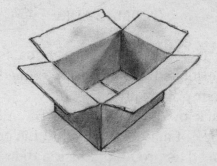

Seven

Curled up in a tight ball, Thistle appeared to be fast asleep. But as Mandy watched, she saw his pointy little face peep out at her. He looked annoyed, like someone woken too soon from a nap.

"Sorry," Mandy whispered, and backed away, taking Blackie with her. He was surprisingly calm and didn't mind in the least being taken away from the leaves he found so irresistible. Instead, he strutted away with a confident air and his head held high. He looked as proud as punch!

James, Grandpa, and Dr. Adam crowded around the pile of leaves, leaning over to see the object of Blackie's excitement. "It *is* Thistle," said Grandpa. Straightening up again, he looked around and beamed at Blackie. "You saved our prickly little friend!"

"In the nick of time, too," said Dr. Adam, and he stuffed the box of matches back into his pocket.

James looked as proud as Blackie did. "What a dog! What a hero!" he declared. He knelt down on the lawn and flung his arms around Blackie. "You're the smartest Labrador in the world. It wasn't the leaves that got you so worked up, was it? You knew Thistle was there and that he was in danger."

Blackie licked James's face.

"He must have smelled the hedgehog," said Dr. Adam. "It's incredible that he tried so hard to warn us."

Grandpa was still peering at Thistle. "That dog's a hedgehog's best friend, all right," he said, turning away at last. "But we're going to have to find a new hibernating spot, somewhere quiet and safe where Thistle can sleep away the winter months. In the meantime, we'll make sure he doesn't burrow down any farther into the leaves." He got a cardboard box from the shed. "I'll hold it open while you pop him in, Mandy."

She bent down and scooped Thistle up along with his leafy blanket. She felt him wriggle, as if in protest. "Sorry," she said, and put him into the box. "I promise we'll find you a much safer winter bed. Do you think we should give him something to eat, Dad?"

"He won't eat anything now that he's so sleepy," said Dr. Adam. "His heartbeat and breathing rate have slowed down so much that he won't have an appetite. And don't forget, he's been eating lots over the past months to build up his fat reserves to carry him through the winter." He closed the flaps on the top of the box. "Come the spring," he continued, "he'll be wide awake again and gobbling all the slugs, snails, and caterpillars he can find."

"That's why I'm so glad he chose my backyard as his home, and why we must make sure he's not harmed," said Grandpa. "He's my very own pest-control agent! Much better than some pesticides that not only kill the pests but poison the wildlife, too." He carried the box to the patio, where he put it on the bench, then tapped on the kitchen window. Gran looked out. "Keep an eye on Thistle," Grandpa said. "He was hibernating in the bonfire pile."

Gran raised her eyebrows. "That was a narrow escape! Who found him?"

"Blackie," James said proudly.

"What a smart dog!" exclaimed Gran. "He deserves a real reward. Bring him in here to me. I have just the thing for him."

It was a leftover can of dog food. "Thistle won't need this now," Gran said to Mandy and James. "So, who better to have it than Blackie?" She spooned it into a dish and put it on the floor. "Enjoy it," she said as Blackie shoved his nose into the dish. "You deserve every last bite."

Standing next to his dog, James's smile was wider than ever.

Grandpa's backyard provided lots of alternative accommodations for a hibernating hedgehog. The hedge was one possibility, also a narrow gap James found between the shed and the greenhouse. Mandy discovered another denlike hole in the undergrowth behind a rainwater barrel next to the garage. In the end, it was the compost heap that got everyone's vote. It was surrounded by corrugated iron walls that would help keep out foxes that sometimes preyed on hedgehogs. Tall shrubs sheltered it from the wind, and it was in a quiet part of the yard, far away from the bonfire heap. Grandpa wouldn't be using it until he started to put out new plants in late spring, so Thistle would be able to sleep undisturbed until the warm weather returned.

"It's perfect," Mandy declared.

Grandpa got a spade and dug a little den at the bottom of the heap. Mandy brought Thistle over and held the box while James opened the lid and took the sleepy creature out.

"He really is prickly," he said when Thistle's spines brushed against his hands. He settled him in his new den, in a bed of grass clippings, while Mandy helped to pack the leaves around him, making him as snug as before.

"I'd like a shot of this," said Grandpa, and he went to get his camera.

After Grandpa had practically filled up his camera's memory card with hedgehog shots, Dr. Adam scooped up an armful of dried grass clippings from the top of the compost heap. He covered Thistle with them. "That should do it," he said. "He's away from prying eyes. But we know where he is, and we can be sure this is where he'll stay until the spring."

"Sleep well, Thistle," Mandy said as they walked away. "See you next year."

This time, it was only a small job to rebuild the leaf pile. When it was ready, Dr. Adam put a match to it at last. Watching the flames dance higher and higher, Mandy thought how close they'd come to lighting it with Thistle trapped inside. Could he have escaped in time? In his sleepy state, would he even have been aware of the fire before it was too late? Then she thought of all the other bonfires around Welford. With all the leaves and branches that had blown down, there would be

dozens and dozens ready to be lit. Surely Grandpa's wouldn't be the only one to attract a hedgehog.

The idea of innocent hedgehogs being burned alive made her declare out loud, "We can't let it happen!"

"Can't let what happen?" said James.

"Other hedgehogs being caught in bonfires. There must be lots of them curled up in piles of leaves," Mandy said. "We've got to do something to save them."

"Like what?" said James.

"We'll figure something out," Mandy said.

When the fire had burned out, they went inside for a snack. Over freshly baked cupcakes, they tossed around ideas for rescuing hedgehogs holed up in bonfire heaps.

"There's not enough time for us to take Blackie to every leaf pile," said James.

"Definitely not," said Dr. Adam. "We need an efficient way of warning lots of people at the same time."

"Like a loudspeaker system," said Grandpa, scrolling through the pictures on his camera.

Gran put a fresh pot of tea on the table. "And where do you think we'd find one of those in a hurry?"

"I don't know," said Grandpa. "I'll ask around."

"In the meantime, lots of hedgehogs are at risk," said Gran, stirring the tea in the pot. "Bonfires are being lit all the time. We've got to move fast."

"A poster warning people to check their leaf piles is probably the easiest thing," said James, eyeing the cupcakes.

Gran pushed the plate across to him. "That might work up to a point. But everyone might not see it in time."

"How about a mass distribution of flyers?" said Dr. Adam. "Like one in every mailbox."

"That's it!" Mandy said. "We could give everyone in Welford their very own flyer with a picture of a hedgehog on it to get their attention."

"A photo of Thistle!" said Gran, peering over Grandpa's shoulder at the camera. "There are dozens of them on here."

Dr. Adam didn't look convinced. "It's a great idea. But we need the job done fast. We can't afford to wait for days while the photograph is being printed onto flyers at the print shop."

"Someone give me strength!" declared Gran. She caught Mandy's eye. "Your father's so out of touch with modern technology. Isn't it time you and James taught him about computers?"

Mandy laughed. "We gave up trying long ago."

Dr. Adam had to go back to Animal Ark for afternoon appointments, but Mandy and James stayed behind to work on the flyer. They used Grandpa's computer, which had all the programs they needed to produce an eye-catching flyer. At the top, in bold red letters, was a warning: HEDGEHOG ALERT! Beneath that was a photograph of Thistle curled up in his new nest.

Grandma helped Mandy and James think of the rest of the wording. Together, they came up with: RIGHT NOW, HEDGEHOGS LIKE THISTLE ARE TUCKING THEMSELVES IN FOR THE WINTER. THEY LIKE SNUG DARK PLACES WITH LOTS OF LEAVES. THERE COULD BE ONE IN YOUR LEAF PILE! PLEASE CHECK BEFORE YOU LIGHT IT. THISTLE'S FRIENDS AND RELATIVES MIGHT JUST BE CURLED UP THERE.

When Grandpa saw the finished product, he was very impressed. "That's great!" he said. "We'll get lots of photocopies done first thing tomorrow, then get on our bikes and deliver one to every house in Welford."

"We'll meet you at the post office after breakfast," Mandy said. But later, as she headed down the road to Animal Ark after she and James had gone their separate ways, it struck her that they would only be scraping the tip of the iceberg. Their flyers might help to secure a second chance for hedgehogs in Welford, but what about all those snuggled up in leaf piles farther away? How could people be warned to look out for them, too?

At dinner, Mandy was still trying to figure out a way to help hedgehogs beyond Welford when Sara phoned.

"Mom and Dad have decided that the PRA information should go in the newspaper after all," she said. "They're going to appeal to the people who took the puppies to be responsible and make sure the condition isn't spread. That way, the thieves might even bring them back."

"I hope so," Mandy said, crossing her fingers.

"The reporter's coming to do an interview around noon tomorrow," said Sara. "Would you like to come over?"

"Sure," Mandy said. It meant she'd have to whiz around the village at top speed, making sure she delivered all her hedgehog flyers first. But there was no way she could miss any opportunity to help find Shan's puppies.

Catherine Taylor, the reporter from the *Walton Gazette*, was a tall, athletic young woman with short black hair, a heart-shaped face, and a tough attitude. "People who steal puppies deserve to be locked up," she said.

Mandy couldn't agree with her more!

"I'll persuade the editor to make it our lead story," said Catherine after the Grants had told her all the details. "We'll need some good photographs, too." She took several of Mr. and Mrs. Grant and Shan, and one or two of Sara kneeling next to the dog. "Some pictures of the puppies would help," she said. "Do you have any?"

"Lots," said Sara, and she gave Catherine her envelope of precious photographs.

Catherine looked through them. "They're such beautiful puppies," she murmured. "And to think they might go blind one day." She chose three photos. "I'll borrow these. They'll definitely get our readers' attention."

Attention! The word gave Mandy a flash of inspiration. "That's just what we need for the hedgehogs!"

"The hedgehogs?" echoed Mr. Grant, giving her a puzzled look.

Mandy opened her backpack and brought out one of the hedgehog flyers. It was the only one left over from their mass delivery. She unrolled it for everyone to see.

"*Hedgehog Alert*," Catherine read aloud. "Animals hibernating in leaf piles!" she exclaimed after reading the rest of the flyer. "The thought never entered my head, but you're right. It's easy to imagine how cozy a pile of leaves would look to a sleepy hedgehog. We have to spread the word."

"I was hoping you would say that," Mandy said. "Do you think there'll be room in your paper for the flyer?"

Catherine took it from Mandy, rolled it up, and put it in her briefcase. "If there isn't, we'll make room," she said. "The timing's just right. It's our special fall-themed issue tomorrow. An article about hedgehogs hibernating fits right in."

Mandy couldn't have hoped for better publicity for the hidden hedgehogs — nor for the stolen puppies. *But will the article be enough?* she wondered when Catherine had left.

As if she knew Mandy was thinking about the puppies, Shan licked her hand.

Mandy stroked the dog's head. She wished she could say with certainty that the puppies would return. But in spite of the publicity they would be getting, the puppies seemed as far away as ever. "We won't stop looking for them," Mandy promised, gazing into Shan's big brown eyes. "Not until they're home with you."

Eight

PUPPIES MIGHT GO BLIND!

The headline on the front page of the *Walton Gazette* practically screamed the shocking news.

Two poignant photographs must have touched the hearts of everyone who saw them. One was of a very sad Shan sitting on the sofa between Mr. and Mrs. Grant, who looked as solemn as could be. The other was a close-up of the puppies peering into Sara's camera lens. They looked so trusting and innocent. *Which makes it even harder to believe anyone could steal them*, Mandy thought.

It was the day after the interview. Mandy had heard the paper land with a thud on the doormat in the hall. She'd been working on her Halloween costume but she dropped it and dashed through to the hall, where she immediately began reading Catherine's article.

The first paragraph dealt with the theft of the puppies, and the next two were about progressive retinal atrophy. *Dogs affected with PRA are programmed to go blind*, Catherine had written. She described how the faulty gene could have been passed on from Ennis to the puppies and that because of this, Verona, Tulip, Alfie, and Berkeley could never be allowed to breed. The article ended with a strong appeal for the puppies to be returned.

Even though Mandy knew all the details, she still felt upset after reading the article. And if *she* was distressed, people who were reading about the puppies for the first time would almost certainly be deeply touched, too.

She took the paper to her mom and dad, who were in one of the treatment rooms studying a set of X-rays taken of a lame pony's back legs. The pictures reminded Mandy of her skeleton costume. She put the newspaper on the desk and Mandy's parents stood together, poring over the article.

"The reporter's done an excellent job," said Dr. Emily. "If the thieves see this, they'll be very worried."

"It doesn't say that the puppies might *not* end up with PRA," said Dr. Adam. "So let's hope the thieves assume the worst, cut their losses, and return all four to the Grants."

And that they don't try to sell them, anyway, Mandy thought. But after reading the *Gazette*, people planning to buy a Labrador puppy would surely want to know where it had come from before they paid for it. In any case, the thieves' luck had to be running out. At least that's what Mandy hoped.

She read the story of the puppies twice, then turned the page to look for Thistle's flyer. It was on the very next page, along with a photograph of Blackie! The caption read, LABRADOR TO THE RESCUE. The story described Blackie's heroic deed and ended with an appeal for everyone to think about hedgehogs before they lit their bonfires. NOT EVERYONE HAS A SMART DOG LIKE BLACKIE! read the final sentence.

"James will be prouder than ever," Mandy said. They'd known that Blackie would appear in the article because Catherine had called James last night and asked him to e-mail her a picture of his dog. But they had no idea that he was going to be made a star! "For once

Blackie's famous for being a hero instead of being the most mischievous dog in town," Mandy joked.

"Which just goes to show," said Dr. Adam with a twinkle in his eye, "that every dog has his day!"

After lunch, Mandy rode her bike to Lilac Cottage. She took the *Walton Gazette* with her just in case Gran and Grandpa hadn't received it. She was going down the sidewalk when the front door opened. Grandpa came out, carrying a rolled-up newspaper.

"Hi, Grandpa," Mandy said, leaning her bike against a lawn chair. "I was wondering if you've . . ."

"Seen the *Gazette*," Grandpa finished. He unrolled the paper. It was the *Gazette*, too. "Great minds think alike." He chuckled. "I was bringing it to show you."

"Is Thistle OK?" Mandy asked. "I mean, is he still in the compost heap?"

"As far as I know," said Grandpa.

"Could we make sure?"

"As long as we're quiet, he probably won't mind," said Grandpa.

They went around to the compost heap, and Mandy peeked over the corrugated iron side. She was relieved to see the grass clippings just as they'd left them. If Thistle had moved, he would have disturbed them. Mandy wasn't satisfied with guessing, though. She reached into her pocket for the stethoscope she had brought from Animal Ark. "We might not be able to see him," she whispered as she put it around her neck and inserted the earpieces, "but we should be able to hear him."

Leaning over the side, she put the stainless steel disk onto the grass clippings and held her breath. A tiny noise, like the faintest tapping on wood, traveled up the hollow tubes to her ears.

Thistle's heartbeat!

Mandy sighed with pleasure. Tucked in his private nest, away from dangerous flames, was one very lucky little hedgehog. And thanks to him and Blackie and Catherine, many more would soon be as safe and snug.

The front page article in the *Gazette* had given Mandy lots of hope that the puppies would suddenly turn up, if not on the Grants' doorstep, then in a place where they'd be quickly spotted. But when there was still no word after two days, and the police had come up with nothing, either, Mandy's hopes started to fade.

Sara was just as depressed. "The house is so empty without the puppies," she said when she phoned Mandy that afternoon. "And it seems even worse now that everyone else has gone and it's just the three of us here."

"Everyone else?" Mandy echoed.

"When there were people working here, they helped to fill the place," Sara explained. "But the landscapers have finished the yard and gone. So has the carpenter. We're not even going to get new carpets now. Mom says she's not in the mood for interior decorating anymore."

After hanging up, Mandy tried to work up some enthusiasm for her skeleton costume. But Halloween and the party seemed so unimportant. She tossed the half-made costume aside and went up to her room. Kicking off her shoes, she flopped down on her bed and flicked through a nature magazine. Outside, the wind had started to blow again. It howled around the eaves and rattled the windowpanes, while outside, the trees, stripped completely of their leaves, groaned and creaked as if in protest.

Those poor puppies! Mandy thought, slamming the magazine down as she pictured them in her mind. They seemed so real, they could have been right in front of her, pleading with her to help them.

"But what else *can* I do?" Mandy sighed. She got up and paced back and forth, racking her brain. *Go door to door asking people? Check out every house for miles around? Phone every pet shop in Yorkshire? See if one of the newspapers in London would carry an article so that millions of people in England would get to see it? Or contact a Web site? Is there one for reporting lost animals?* Of them all, the last seemed a possibility. "James will know how to find out," she said. She charged downstairs to call him but the phone was already ringing.

She picked it up. "Animal Ark. Mandy Hope speaking."

"Ah, just the person I'm looking for," said a gruff voice at the other end.

It was Lydia Fawcett, a farmer who lived at High Cross Farm along with her herd of goats. Reserved and sometimes a bit bad-tempered, Lydia nevertheless had a heart of gold — especially when it came to her beloved animals.

"Hi, Lydia," Mandy said. "Is everything OK with the goats?"

"Just fine," said Lydia, her fondness for them coming through in her softer tone, "but it's not them I'm calling about. You see, I was out in the field just now, trying to catch Houdini." Houdini was a billy goat who, like his famous namesake, was a brilliant escape artist. "We were coming back down the trail when we spotted something in the ditch," continued Lydia. "Turned out to be three puppies."

"Puppies!" Mandy's heart skipped a beat, but sank

almost right away. Lydia said three. Not four. "What breed? And how old?"

"Two months, maybe," said Lydia. "And they look like Labradors to me — buttery color, sweet faces, short hair. I was wondering if they might be those pups I read about in the *Gazette*, the ones that have been stolen."

Mandy's hopes soared again. Yellow Labradors, about the same age as Shan's puppies! "I hope they are," she said. "We'll be right there."

A few minutes later, Mandy and her mom were on their way to High Cross Farm, taking with them a can of specially formulated milk for puppies. "It's *got* to be them," Mandy said over and over again. *How many Labrador puppies disappear, and all at the same time?* she told herself, every time she remembered that Lydia had said there were just three.

"Don't get your hopes too high," her mom warned as they drove along the rutted track to High Cross Farm. It was a tiny place perched on a hill. Stunted hawthorn trees sheltered it. Today, though, they provided little protection. The wind battered them as if they were nothing more than twigs and roared through their gnarled branches to slam against the walls and windows of the old stone farmhouse where Lydia lived.

Dr. Emily swerved to avoid a pothole. "Even if they're not Shan's puppies," she went on, "they must be lost. So they need our help, too."

Lydia was waiting for them in front of the house. She was a small-framed woman of about fifty with short gray hair. Her baggy clothes had been patched so often that even the patches had been mended many times. Houdini, big, black and white, and with the sassiest expression Mandy had ever seen on a goat, was in a nearby stable. He looked out over the door, energetically chewing a bundle of straw.

"I'm glad you could come so quickly," said Lydia, ushering them in through the red front door. "The poor little things are starving. They've been snuffling about in the box and whining. I'd have given them goat's milk but I'm not sure if they can have it."

"It's best not to . . ." Dr. Emily began as they entered the kitchen.

Mandy didn't hear anything else. Right in front of her, in a high-sided cardboard box lined with a towel, a litter of Labrador puppies peered out. Three, not four puppies, nearly identical and as typically Labrador as any Lab, but totally familiar to Mandy. If there was any doubt in her mind at all, it vanished the moment she noticed the yellow satin ribbon around one puppy's neck. *Yellow ribbon = Tulip.*

"It's them!" she cried, covering the last few feet toward them in one giant step. She dropped onto her knees, leaned into the box, and threw her arms around them. "You're safe," she said, tears flowing down her cheeks.

"So they *are* the puppies mentioned in the paper?" said Lydia. "I thought so."

Mandy didn't look up. She was too busy cuddling the furry bundles in the box, and she was also very worried. Wet and muddy, the puppies trembled with cold.

But something even worse was troubling Mandy. "One's still missing," she said, finally looking up.

"Which one?" asked Dr. Emily, crouching beside her.

Mandy looked closely at the three. Only Tulip was wearing her ribbon. Perhaps the thieves had taken the others off and overlooked Tulip's because it was nearly the same color as her coat. But Mandy no longer needed the ribbons. Knowing their characters, she could tell the puppies apart as easily as she knew the difference between day and night. "This is Verona," she said, giving the other little female a hug. She patted the third, the biggest of the three. "And this is Berkeley." She felt fresh tears running down her cheeks as she answered her mom's question. "It's Alfie. We've *got* to go look for him, too."

"We must get these three back to Shan first," said Dr. Emily. "Just as soon as I've checked them to see if they're all right."

Lydia bent down, her hands resting on her knees. "They were even dirtier when I found them. I tried to wipe off some of the mud, but you can see how thick their coats are with it. They must have been in that ditch for a long time."

"Thank goodness Houdini decided to escape today," Mandy said.

"Indeed," said Dr. Emily as she felt Tulip's tummy.

Mandy saw with a pang that it was no longer a tummy plump with good food, but thin and rumbling with hunger.

Dr. Emily checked all three puppies and announced that, apart from being a little underweight, they were fine. "We'll give them some food before we take them home," she said.

"So you'll need some milk?" asked Lydia, reaching for a jug on the table.

"Actually, we brought some special formula," said Dr. Emily. "We just need a jug of boiled water and a dish."

The water in the kettle had been boiled not too long before so Mandy poured out the right amount into the jug then heaped in the powdered formula and stirred it until it was dissolved. Lydia found a wide shallow dish that was perfect for a litter of puppies sharing a drink, and Mandy poured the formula into it.

When they were put in front of the bowl, the puppies barely sniffed it to find out what was inside. In less than a minute, they'd lapped up the formula, leaving the bowl licked clean. Berkeley and Verona sniffed around, looking for more, but Tulip claimed the dish as her own. She planted her front paws in it and looked up at everyone with a satisfied doggy grin on her face. Specks of milk dotted her muzzle. She tried to lick them off but couldn't make her tongue reach far enough.

"You enjoyed that, didn't you?" Mandy said, scooping her up to put her in the box while Lydia and Dr. Emily picked up the other two and put them in with their sister, ready for their journey home.

Mandy had a busy time on the drive to the Grants' house. She sat in the backseat with the puppies in their box next to her. Now that they weren't hungry anymore, they were very lively, clambering around and wrestling with one another. They kept standing up against the sides of the box, and Mandy was busy trying to stop them from climbing out.

But she wasn't too busy to stop worrying that Alfie wasn't going to make it home with his sisters and brother.

At the Grants' house, Dr. Emily had just turned off the engine when Sara came outside. She looked puzzled as she walked to the Land Rover. "Hi, Mandy. I thought you said that you were staying home this afternoon."

Mandy was sitting twisted sideways, with both hands in the box to keep the puppies in. Dr. Emily got out and came around to help her. Sara came up beside her just as Mandy's mom opened the back door and stretched across to pick up the box.

"What's in . . ." she began, but she broke off as she stared past Dr. Emily. Her eyes stretched wide and she stood openmouthed as Mandy's mom lifted out the precious cargo.

Mandy shuffled along the seat behind the box until she reached the door. She jumped down in front of Sara, who was trying to speak but couldn't seem to find the words.

"I . . . where . . . I mean, how . . . who . . ." She gasped, and then she was laughing and crying both at once and reaching into the box to gather the puppies into her arms.

Yipping with excitement, the baby Labradors bounced around, scrabbling at Sara's hands. Still laughing through her tears, she bent over to kiss the tops of their heads before looking up just long enough to call out, "Mom, Dad, come quickly. And bring Shan," and then she was hugging the puppies again. Suddenly, she looked up at Mandy. There was a frantic look in her eyes. "Where's —" she began but she was interrupted by Mrs. Grant calling out, "What's going on?" as she came rushing out with Sara's dad, both of them looking worried, as if they expected to find Sara in some kind of trouble.

Shan raced over, too, but stopped dead just a few feet from Mandy and Sara. She pricked up her ears and put her head to one side, listening. It took just one faint *yap* for her to recognize the voice of one of her babies. With a jubilant bark, she bounded over to them and sprang up on her hind legs to see where they were.

"Just a moment," said Dr. Emily, and she and Mandy carefully lowered the box to the ground.

Knowing their mother instantly, the little Labradors jumped up at Shan's face. They licked her mouth and pawed at her cheeks, whining with excitement. Shan sniffed them one by one, checking them over, trying to figure out where they'd been and, Mandy was sure, counting them to see they were all there.

This made Mandy swallow uncomfortably. Then Shan looked up at Mandy, her forehead wrinkled in a frown, and she knew that Shan had noticed.

One of her puppies wasn't in the box.

Nine

"It's not all good news," Mandy told James when she called him a little while later on her mom's cell phone.

"It isn't?"

"No." Mandy watched the puppies chasing a ball that Sara had rolled across the floor. Shan sat at Mandy's feet. She looked much happier, even though she must have felt that a part of her was still missing. "Alfie never made it home."

"No!" said James.

"Mom thinks he could have been sold before the thieves found out about the PRA," Mandy continued. She thought about the time Alfie had tumbled off Shan's back to land on the floor with his little legs sticking up in the air. The memory made her smile. "He *was* sort of special."

Sara looked sadly at Mandy. "The type of puppy that gets snapped up fast," she murmured.

"What if he wasn't sold?" said James. "What if he was dumped with the others and is still in that ditch?"

"Lydia said she definitely saw only three puppies," Mandy said. "And there was no way they could have climbed out on their own."

"He *can't* have been sold," said James, as if he was trying to convince himself. "And we're not giving up yet."

Mandy was still talking to James when Mrs. Grant brought in some food for the puppies. She put the bowl down and they charged over to it.

"Take it easy," said Sara as they wolfed it down, not even pausing to take a breath.

Mandy closed her eyes for a moment. She pictured Alfie, hungry, alone, missing his siblings, frightened and helpless.

"What we have to do now," James was saying, "is find where they were being kept. There's every chance that Alfie escaped. And if he did get out, he couldn't have gone all that far. His legs aren't exactly long."

"They could have been kept just about anywhere,"

Mandy said gloomily. Miles and miles of fields surrounded Walton and Welford. There was no shortage of places to hide a litter of puppies. "It'll be like looking for a needle in a haystack," she continued. "It was pure luck that Lydia saw the puppies. How often do people even go that way?"

"Precisely," said James. "That's why I think the puppies were being kept near Lydia's place. It's so remote that no one would have heard them, and the chances of anyone seeing them would have been zilch, too."

This made sense — like most of James's ideas. "So what are you waiting for?" Mandy said. "You need to get over here fast so we can get to High Cross Farm before dark."

The wind had dropped but daylight was fading when Mandy, James, and Sara pedaled breathlessly up the track to High Cross Farm. Blackie trotted next to James, who kept him on his leash in case he saw a rabbit and took off. Earlier, James's dad had dropped him and Blackie at Sara's house, along with his bike and Mandy's, which they'd picked up from Animal Ark.

They found Lydia in the barn, settling the goats in for the night. Bending over a cardboard box in front of a stall, she had her back to the door when the three friends entered. Blackie was outside, tied up to a fence post.

"Hi, Lydia," Mandy said.

Lydia shot upright and spun around. "Phew!" she exclaimed when she saw them. "You gave me such a scare." She patted her chest.

"Sorry," Mandy said.

"We should have knocked first," said Sara.

"No, no," said Lydia. "It's just that I wasn't expecting visitors." She half turned and, with one foot, kicked the flaps of the box over the top, closing it. Then she nudged it along the ground until it was some way back from the pen. "It's not often people come here, let alone drop in twice in one day."

"My point exactly," said James, which made Lydia give him a puzzled look. "Mandy told you about the missing puppy, didn't she?"

Lydia nodded as she picked bits of straw off her baggy brown sweater.

"Well, we think he's around here somewhere," said James.

"Here?" Lydia crossed her arms and narrowed her eyes. "You're not suggesting I stole him?"

"Of course not!" said James. "We'd *never* think that." He glanced at the goat closest to him, a young nanny goat who was in such good condition, her brown coat shone. "But we think the thieves hid them in the area, somewhere people hardly ever go."

"Humph!" muttered Lydia, and turned back to the goat she'd been attending to. "So you're going to search for that puppy?" She picked up a bucket of water and filled the drinking pail that was just outside the pen. There was an opening in the gate big enough for a goat's head to fit through so they could reach the water, but without being able to kick the pail over. "You'll be lucky if you find him."

"We have to try," said Sara. "We were wondering if you know of anywhere nearby that people could use as a hideout."

Lydia moved on to the next stall, kicking the box in front of her. A white kid goat greeted her with a happy bleat. "A hideout? Hmm. Let me see." She stroked the back of the kid's neck. "You mean, like a derelict house or an old barn?"

"Maybe," Mandy said.

The kid nibbled at Lydia's sleeve. She didn't seem to notice. She stared ahead, lost in thought. "I don't think anyone would risk sneaking onto Sam Western's land," she said eventually. Sam was a wealthy dairy farmer and Lydia's closest neighbor. He was also an unpleasant man with a ruthless attitude. "But you might try

Symes's Cottage." She looked down to see the kid trying to eat her sleeve. "Rascal!" she scolded, tapping his nose.

"Where's that?" James prompted.

Lydia examined a ragged hole in her sweater that was the size of an egg. She clicked her tongue. "Rats! More darning," she said, then to James, "You don't know Symes's?"

"Nope," said James, and Mandy and Sara shook their heads, too.

"It's a vacation cottage a couple of miles away." Lydia bent down and opened the box. It was full of apples. She took one out and gave it to the young goat. "There, that's better than an old woolly sleeve, isn't it, my beauty?"

"A couple of miles in which direction?" said James, sounding impatient.

Lydia pointed to the back wall of the barn. "In the woods in the valley down yonder. There's a path across the field — the one I led Houdini along yesterday — that joins into the main trail to the place." She picked up the bucket and splashed water into the kid's drinking pail. "I've heard the cottage is popular with city folk on account of it being so quiet. But I can't say if anyone's staying there right now. Come September, the place is usually empty until spring."

"That's it! The perfect hideout!" said James, punching

his fist into the palm of his other hand. He jerked his head toward the door. "Let's check it out." And without waiting for Mandy and Sara, he raced out of the barn.

Looking down at the valley, Mandy could see only the dark green of closely packed pine trees. It looked very gloomy, especially with dusk approaching. "We have to hurry," she said, "or we won't be able to see where we're going."

They rode their bikes down the winding path, bumping over stones and tufts of grass. Blackie ran next to them, his tail straight out and his nose close to the ground. He looked every inch a working dog, out on the chase.

"Forget rabbits," James warned him, "and even hedgehogs. You're looking for your own kind this time." But when Blackie suddenly tore after a crow flying westward, James shook his head. "I suppose he can't always be a hero."

Farther along, the path became very overgrown, but even so, Mandy spotted a deep ditch at the side. "This must be where Lydia found them," she said, getting off her bike to look into the ditch. Scrape marks on the sides, and paw prints in the mud at the bottom, told her she was right. "What a horrible place to leave three helpless puppies," she said, shivering at the thought of them trapped in there.

James and Sara peered into it, too. "Even though Alfie loved to climb, he definitely wouldn't have been able to get out of this," said Sara. "It's much too deep."

"Then let's not waste any more time here," said James.

At the bottom of the hill, the path led them along the side of a stream. James clipped on Blackie's leash in case he decided to go for a dip. "No time for swimming now," he said.

About a hundred yards farther, the path merged with a wider trail that ran at a right angle to it, the one Lydia had told them about. Fresh tire marks suggested that they were on the way to their destination.

"We'll leave the bikes here so that we can move quietly," said James, stashing his behind a bush. "Just in case someone's still at the cottage."

Mandy and Sara did the same. Blackie must have understood he had to be quiet, too. He padded along next to James, for once not pulling on the leash.

The cottage blended so well with its surroundings, it would have been easy to miss it in the dark. An ivy-covered wooden fence surrounded it, and it was only when they went through the gate that they could see the little house properly. Built of gray stone and with a slate-tiled roof, it stood in a leaf-strewn garden. More leaves were piled up on the front porch and against the walls, and a fallen branch blocked the entrance to a carport on one side. The doors and windows were closed, and the curtains drawn.

"It doesn't *look* like anyone's here," said Sara.

Mandy agreed. There was a bleakness about the place that reminded her of a seaside cottage boarded up for the winter. She started up the steps to the front door, but James grabbed her arm. "Wait," he whispered. "We can't be sure no one's here."

"There's no car," Mandy argued.

"That doesn't mean a thing," James insisted.

They crept around the side of the house, looking for gaps in the curtains they could peek through and listening for sounds from inside. A steady *drip, drip, drip* made them stop dead until James pointed to a tap next to the back door. Water plopped out of it onto a crumpled blue plastic bag caught in the drain below.

Mandy turned the tap off. She picked up the plastic bag, meaning to put it in a garbage can if she found one. It was soaking wet and dripped against her so she held it at arm's length and shook it. Straightened out, it revealed the name of a store. In bold black lettering, the slogan read: MOORLANDS PET SUPPLIES — FOR ALL YOUR PET'S NEEDS.

"James! Sara!" Mandy hissed. They were at the back door, peeking through the glass panel that made up the top half. Blackie stood next to James, as good as gold.

"What?" said James, looking over his shoulder.

Mandy held up the bag.

"Aha!" James said, putting his hands on his hips. "The plot thickens."

Sara looked around, one hand resting on the door handle.

Suddenly, the door opened!

They all jumped. "Golly!" exclaimed James, while Sara gasped out loud. Mandy held her breath, waiting for someone to burst out and demand to know what they were doing there. But no one came. Whoever had gone out last must have forgotten to lock the door. It had only needed Sara to lean on the handle for it to open.

"Let's look inside," James whispered. Keeping Blackie on a short leash, he led the way into a cramped, old-fashioned kitchen. There was a red plastic dish on the floor in one corner, half-filled with water. Nearby on the wall, just a few inches from the floor, were three or four brown smudges. They were exactly like paw prints! Puppy paw prints. Mandy could almost picture one of Shan's puppies jumping up against the wall with muddy feet.

They tiptoed to the door on the other side of the kitchen, pausing to peer into the darkened room in front of them. Silence greeted them, and nothing moved in the shadows.

"Definitely no one here," Mandy decided, boldness making her talk out loud. She went through the door and felt around the wall until she found a light switch. She flicked it on and saw they were in the living room. The curtains were drawn and the room was sparsely furnished with a sofa, a single armchair, and two side tables. There was a newspaper on one of the tables. "I bet that's the *Gazette*," Mandy said, and went to check.

It wasn't. It was a weekend newspaper, the date showing it was almost a week old.

"At least we know there were people here recently," said Sara.

James was fishing around in a wastepaper basket. He held up something. "Bingo!" he said. Two ribbons dangled from his hand: one green, the other red.

Verona's and Berkeley's ribbons! It was the most solid clue so far. Only one ribbon was missing now. The blue one.

Alfie had to be somewhere close by.

They searched every nook and cranny, behind doors, under the stairs, in cupboards and drawers, and even in the tiny attic. Finding nothing, they went into the yard again. Blackie found lots of interesting smells and pulled James back and forth, but none of the invisible trails led to the missing puppy.

Dusk was gathering, and Mandy was afraid they

would soon have to abandon the search until morning. "There *has* to be another clue around here," she said. She checked the ground next to the carport, hoping to see at least one paw print. Finding none, she straightened up and noticed pink paint on one of the metal poles that held up the roof.

She called James and Sara. "It looks like someone scraped a pink car against this pole."

James wrinkled his nose. "A blob of paint's hardly a clue."

"It is if it's from the thieves' car," Mandy pointed out. "There can't be many pink cars around."

"I guess not," agreed James. "The only one I know is Carole's van."

"Carole?" Sara echoed.

"She owns a bakery called Carole's Cakes," Mandy said. "But there's no way she'd steal puppies."

"I still don't think a splotch of paint's going to lead us to the thieves," said James. Blackie was straining at his leash, trying to pull James over to the fence. "OK, I'm coming," said James, and he broke into a run as Blackie powered his way across the backyard. At the fence, Blackie skidded to a stop. A moment later, James called out, "Hey! This is more like it."

Mandy and Sara ran over. Blackie had found a gap in the fence. It was just big enough for a puppy to fit through!

What was more, there was a tuft of hair caught on the wood. It was yellow, exactly the color of the puppies' fur.

"Let's go!" said James, and they sprinted to the gate.

On the other side of the fence, Blackie picked up a scent at once and followed it into the woods. "We'll have to trust that it's a puppy scent and not a rabbit trail," puffed James.

Blackie zigzagged ahead. Gripping the leash in both hands and running to keep up with his dog, James could have been on a cross-country race. He had to jump over logs and mud puddles, duck under low branches, and swerve to avoid trees.

Close behind, Mandy and Sara paused once or twice to look at marks on the ground in case they were paw prints. But it was only when they came to a narrow, fast-flowing river that Mandy found a tiny footprint of an animal on the muddy bank. "Definitely a dog's paw print," she said when she bent down for a closer look. There were four or five others close by, faint indents, but clear enough for Mandy to see that they all led toward the swift black water!

No. Not that, Mandy thought, and looked up in time to see Sara wince as she stared at the swirling river. She must have feared what Mandy did — that Alfie had fallen in and been swept away.

Mandy only had to look at Blackie to confirm her misgivings. As if the trail had suddenly gone cold, he stood looking into the water. James looked both puzzled and worried.

"You don't think Alfie's . . ." Mandy couldn't bring herself to say any more.

"I don't know what to —" James didn't finish his sentence, either, because suddenly Blackie let out a loud *woof,* jerked the leash out of James's hand, and shot off along the riverbank.

"Now what?" said James.

"He must be on the scent again," Mandy said, but her heart dropped when she saw what Blackie was really after.

It was a heap of leaves blown up against a tree. Red, yellow, gold, and orange, the vibrant fall colors stood out clearly even in the fading light. It must have been an irresistible sight for a dog crazy about leaves.

"Not again," groaned James.

They ran to Blackie, reaching him just as he started batting the leaves with his front paws. "This is no time for games," said James, pulling him away.

Just then, the heap of leaves shifted. It looked as if something was pushing it up from underneath.

"It could be a mole. Or another hedgehog," James said, curiously watching the heaving leaves.

Suddenly, they parted and a little head popped out. A creamy-yellow head.

It was no mole — not even a hedgehog.

There was a *Labrador* in the leaves.

"Alfie!" Mandy shouted.

Ten

With Alfie tucked safely inside Sara's jacket, the three friends hurried away from Symes's Cottage. They paused at High Cross Farm just long enough to tell Lydia the good news, then rode on again at top speed. They reached Animal Ark and burst into the clinic just as Mandy's parents were locking up for the night.

"There you are!" said Dr. Adam, sounding annoyed. "We were getting very worried about you. You all should have been home hours ago."

"We found Alfie!" Mandy blurted out while Sara

unzipped her jacket to reveal the puppy snuggled up against her.

Dr. Adam looked astonished. "Where was he?"

While Mandy described their expedition to Symes's Cottage, the two vets checked to see if Alfie was all right. "He's thin like the others," said Dr. Emily when she'd finished examining him, "and probably very hungry. But otherwise, he's in great shape."

Sara's smile couldn't have been wider. But as she bent to pick up Alfie and he blinked up at her, a shadow of sadness crossed her face. "He's fine now," she murmured, hugging him close, "but no one can say for how long." She bit her lip. "I can't believe the puppies might all go blind."

Dr. Emily put her arm around her. "It's tough to think about that, I know," she said. "But it's better that we know they're at risk. At least this way the new owners will be prepared if their dogs do go blind."

"And it's thanks to Lydia and the three of you that the owners *will* know," said Dr. Adam. "If the thieves had sold them, they probably wouldn't have told the new owners about the PRA."

Blackie had been lying on the floor, exhausted after his busy afternoon. He sat up suddenly and barked at Dr. Adam.

"I *do* apologize," said Dr. Adam, winking at Mandy. "How could I have forgotten the real hero?"

Blackie barked again and looked up at the hedgehog flyer that Mandy had hung on the wall a few days earlier.

"He's trying to remind us of something else," Mandy said.

"That he's not a modest hero?" teased Dr. Adam, patting Blackie.

James chuckled. "No. That he's a two-time hero."

A little while later, after Blackie had been dropped off at home to enjoy his reward of a bunch of doggy treats, there was a second heartwarming reunion at the Grants' house. Shan couldn't stop licking Alfie, who squirmed and protested like any little boy who found himself being smothered in love.

Mr. and Mrs. Grant were very relieved to have Alfie back safe and sound. "It was a nightmare not knowing what had happened to him," said Mrs. Grant.

When the puppies, worn out after some serious playing, were curled up with Shan, the humans celebrated with steaming cups of hot chocolate.

Mr. Grant raised his mug. "I propose a toast."

They all lifted their mugs.

"To the three of you," said Mr. Grant, looking at Mandy, James, and Sara, "but also, and most especially" — he paused — "to Blackie."

"To Blackie!" everyone echoed while James looked as if he'd burst with pride.

Alfie's homecoming wasn't the only good thing to happen that day. "There was a call earlier this evening from the people who wanted to buy Verona," said Mrs. Grant as she handed around a plate of cookies. "They're not worried that she might go blind, and they never intended to breed her. They said they definitely

want to have her and will love her no matter what happens."

Sara's eyes shone. "Wonderful! That's exactly the kind of home we want for the puppies."

"There were two other calls today," said Mr. Grant more solemnly. "One was from the people who wanted Tulip, and the other from a family that was going to take Berkeley. They'd seen the article in the *Gazette* and wanted to know if the puppies had been found yet."

"And?" Sara prompted.

Mandy saw Mr. and Mrs. Grant trade a fleeting look before Mr. Grant continued. "They both canceled. They said they'd rather buy healthy puppies."

"They *are* healthy," protested Sara, looking outraged.

"But not everyone is prepared to put up with a blind dog one day," her mom pointed out.

There was a moment's silence before Sara said, "Well, it's their loss." And although she was cheerful for the rest of the evening, sadness must have been brewing inside her all along. For later, when Mandy and her parents and James were leaving, there was no sign of Sara.

"She's probably checking on Shan and the puppies," said Mrs. Grant.

"I'll just say good-bye to her," Mandy said, and went through to the puppy nursery.

She found Sara stroking the sleeping puppies and crying quietly. "It'll be okay," Mandy said, crouching down beside her.

Sara looked up at her with tears spilling out of her eyes. "No one wants them anymore," she sobbed. "It's horrible to think of them ending up blind with no one to love them."

"But Verona's going to a great home," Mandy said. "That's a start." She knew it was hardly a comforting reply. With two people canceling, no one else waiting in line for the puppies, and the threat of blindness hanging over them, the future for Alfie, Tulip, and Berkeley was looking very bleak.

"Shouldn't you be working on your Halloween costume?" Dr. Emily asked Mandy the next morning after breakfast.

It was the last Saturday of midterm, two days before the Halloween party. Mandy was getting ready to go out. "No time for that now," she said, pulling on her gloves. "We're going to find out who stole the puppies."

"How do you propose to do that?" asked Dr. Adam, looking up from his newspaper.

"Easy," Mandy said. "Lydia knows the owner of Symes's Cottage. We're going to ask him about the people who were staying there."

The owner, Ian Higgins, was a stationmaster who had recently retired to Welford. He lived behind the Fox and Goose restaurant and had bought Symes's Cottage as an investment. "Why are you so interested in the place?" he asked after he invited them in to his tiny living room.

Sara told him about the puppies being stolen and how they'd found Alfie near the cottage.

"We're ninety-nine point nine percent sure the people who stole them were staying there," James added.

Mr. Higgins was taken aback. "Never! The nicest couple rented Symes's about a month ago. Paid cash up front even before they saw the place. Said they just wanted somewhere peaceful for a couple of weeks."

"What were their names?" Mandy asked.

Mr. Higgins thought for a moment. "Howard," he finally said, and, after another pause, "Jake and, er, Katie . . . no, that's not it, Cara, no, Karen. That's it. Karen."

"Jake and Karen Howard," said James. "Doesn't sound familiar. Do you know where they were from?"

Mr. Higgins cupped his chin in his hand. "Let me

see. . . . Did they ever say? Hmmm . . . Can't say I remember." He drummed his cheek with one finger. "Sorry," he said eventually. "I really can't recall."

Disappointed to have come to a dead end, the three friends turned to go. But just before he reached the door, James stopped. "What did they look like?" he asked.

"Who?" said Mr. Higgins.

"The Howards," said James, and before Mr. Higgins could reply, he added, "Was the man tall with dark hair and a tanned face, and the woman tall, too, with short blond hair?"

Mandy was puzzled. Where did James get these descriptions? And yet something about them struck a chord. Did *she* know people who looked like that?

Mr. Higgins took off his eyeglasses and chewed on one of the tips while staring straight ahead. "Tall, tan face, dark hair, the woman tall with short blond hair?" he echoed slowly. "Well," he said at last, putting his glasses back on, "that sums them up exactly."

"Yes!" exclaimed James at the same time that Sara gasped, "The landscapers!"

A heartbeat later, Mandy said, "Of course!" James had described Peter and Faye Cole, the Gorgeous Gardens team who'd been designing the Grants' garden. "They knew all about the puppies being well-bred. Remember all their questions?" she said.

"Not just that," said James. "You were right about that pink paint, Mandy. It didn't come from a pink car, but from a van with pink flowers painted on it!"

"Peter and Faye's van," said Sara.

Mr. Higgins, shocked that his cottage had been used as a thieves' hideout, said they had to report the matter to the police at once. So they went back inside, and Mandy called her mom.

Shortly afterward, Dr. Emily arrived to drive them all to the Walton police station. There, they made a statement and gave the police the real names of the gardening team.

"They're probably not even real landscape designers," Mandy said.

The police officer agreed. "They could be a con team posing as gardeners." He came out from behind his desk and shook their hands. "Excellent work, all of you," he said. Smiling, he added, "If you're thinking of becoming detectives when you graduate, come back and see me!"

With the case all but closed, Mandy could finally concentrate on her Halloween costume. Back home, she had just started to work on the half-completed skeleton outfit when the phone rang. Mandy's parents were relaxing in the living room, so Mandy went to take the call.

The caller was Catherine Taylor, the reporter from the *Walton Gazette*. "I thought you'd like to know that the hedgehog article was a huge hit," she told Mandy. "We've had dozens of e-mails and calls from people who checked their leaf piles and made sure their neighbors and friends did the same."

"Terrific!" Mandy said. She felt a glow of happiness as she thought of all the hedgehogs that had been saved. After she hung up, she went to her mom and dad. "Operation Thistle is a success," she said, and repeated what Catherine had told her.

"Another job well done," Dr. Emily said. "What's your next project?"

"Actually, that's about to start now," said Dr. Adam, putting down his book. "Get your coat, Mandy, and call James and Sara. Tell them to be ready in five minutes."

"For what?"

"That would be telling," her dad said. "Just say we're going on a surprise trip."

During the drive to the mystery destination, Mandy, James, and Sara kept prodding Dr. Adam to tell them where they were going. "Is it early trick-or-treating?" James guessed.

"Nope," said Dr. Adam.

"You've taken us prisoner so we have to listen to you at choir practice in some cold and drafty hall," Mandy said.

"You volunteered us to rake up leaves on the school athletic fields," suggested Sara, smiling.

Mandy's dad just shook his head and didn't say anything. On the outskirts of Walton, he turned into a driveway and parked in front of a ranch-style bungalow. "You're about to meet Olivia Moult," he announced.

"Who is she?" asked James as they all climbed out.

"A wonderful person," said Dr. Adam, knocking on the door.

A jingling, like small bells ringing, sounded from inside and then the door opened. A woman about the same age as Mandy's mom greeted them warmly. "How lovely to see you all. Come in, come in," she said, stepping aside to let them enter.

"This is Mrs. Moult, everyone," said Dr. Adam.

"Call me Olivia, please," she said. She was petite and had big green eyes and curly auburn hair that fell softly to her shoulders. "Mrs. Moult sounds so stuffy, especially among friends. And we *are* going to be great friends. Especially Sara and me."

"Oh?" said Sara.

"Yes, of course," said Olivia. "We have a lot in common. You have Alfie. . . ."

"Actually, he's not mine," said Sara. "He's for sale, like Shan's other puppies."

Olivia seemed surprised. "Oh, I see. I thought . . ." She shrugged and closed the door. "Never mind. We still have lots to talk about. But that can come later. Neptune can't wait to meet you."

"Neptune?" Mandy echoed.

"My dog," Olivia explained, leading them through the hall.

The bells started jingling again. The sound seemed to come from the floor. Looking down, Mandy saw that Olivia was wearing slippers with a bell on each toe. *That's really weird*, she thought, and shot a glance at James. He widened his eyes to show his surprise, too. But in the very next moment, Mandy forgot all about Olivia's odd footwear. A big black Labrador had appeared in a doorway ahead of them. "What a gorgeous dog!" she gasped.

"My lovely boy, Neptune," Olivia said proudly.

Neptune trotted straight toward them, his tail wagging so fast, it would have knocked over anything in its way.

"Hi, Neptune," Mandy said, and put her hand out. But he seemed to ignore her, sniffing the air to one side. It was for only a moment, though, because he was soon sniffing her fingers and licking them with his velvety tongue.

James and Sara put their hands out, too. Like with Mandy, Neptune ignored them at first. Instead he looked up at Mandy, giving her a wide doggy grin when she said, "You're such a handsome boy." Except he didn't look at her face, but to one side of her, past her shoulder as if there were someone behind her. She glanced back and saw no one, and when she looked to the front again, Neptune was sniffing James up and down.

Suddenly, the pieces started fitting together. The way Neptune seemed to use his nose so much, the inaccurate direction of his gaze, the way he'd ignored James's and Sara's hands, the bells on his owner's slippers . . .

"Neptune's *blind*!" she exclaimed.

"Yes, of course," said Olivia. "Didn't you know?"

"Dad!" Mandy said. "You should have told us."

"I was going to," he said, "but then I thought you should see that a blind dog can lead a perfectly normal life — even before you knew the dog was blind."

Hearing another friendly human voice, Neptune checked Dr. Adam over in the same "nosy" way. He seemed to take a shine to him, leaping up to rest his paws against Dr. Adam's thighs. He was a powerful dog, with well-developed muscles and a deep, wide body, and he must have weighed a lot, judging by the way Mandy's dad had to brace himself so he wouldn't lose his balance.

Mandy grinned. "You've got a new fan."

Dr. Adam patted Neptune's neck. "We're old friends. We go back a long way, don't we, Neptune?"

The dog barked.

"It's been, what, two years since we diagnosed progressive retinal atrophy, Olivia?" said Dr. Adam.

PRA! The same as Ennis, the puppies' father. Mandy glanced at Sara and saw that she couldn't take her eyes off Neptune.

"Yes, two years since I first noticed that his pupils were dilated even in daylight and that he was having trouble seeing in the dark," said Olivia. "And in that time, he's gradually gone completely blind. But as you can see, it doesn't bother him in the least. He's as happy as the day I first got him. In fact, he's gone from strength to strength. We had to make a few adjustments, of course. . . ." She jiggled her foot, making the bell jingle, then smiled at Mandy and James and Sara. "Neptune thinks these are great because he always knows where I am, but you probably thought I was nutty."

Mandy smiled sheepishly. "I *did* wonder," she admitted. "I mean, it's not like the latest fashion or anything."

They spent the rest of the afternoon with Olivia and Neptune, seeing for themselves the adjustments Olivia had mentioned. For one thing, she never changed the way the furniture was arranged. "He knows where things are in every room," said Olivia. "That means he can find his way around and doesn't bump into things."

As if to demonstrate, Neptune strolled confidently past them to his bed in the corner of the living room. He picked up a rubber ball that, like Olivia's slippers, jingled.

"I bet that's so he can locate it when someone throws it for him!" said Sara.

"You got it," said Olivia, looking pleased that Sara had noticed.

While they had some snacks, she explained that she made sure Neptune's water bowl was always in the same place, and that she left a radio on most of the time to help him get his bearings. "I also made sure that there are no sharp edges anywhere indoors where he could poke his eyes," she added. "And the same outdoors, with twigs and branches and spiky plants."

They were very simple adjustments, Mandy realized, things that anyone could do. But they made a world of difference to a blind dog. And just when Mandy thought she'd seen it all, Olivia brought out the most amazing thing. It was a soft fabric harness that Neptune wore around his chest and attached to it was a sturdy plastic hoop that jutted out in front, a little farther than his nose. The hoop stopped him from bumping into objects he didn't know were in front of him. It meant he could go out for walks, even to new places, and explore his surroundings safely.

"It's so cool!" said James as they watched Neptune demonstrate his hoop in the backyard. Just for the exercise, Olivia had moved a lawn chair to the middle of the yard. Neptune headed straight for it but stopped when he felt the hoop bang into it and press gently on his chest. "It's the canine version of a white cane," James said when Neptune took a detour around the seat.

When it was time to leave, Sara thanked Olivia for showing her that blindness didn't have to ruin a dog's life. "Neptune's one of the happiest dogs I've ever met," she said. "I feel a whole lot better now because I know that even if our puppies end up blind, they'll be just fine."

"We can make doubly sure they will by writing up a list of all the things their new families can do," Mandy said. It would be her first job when she got home that evening.

"*If* we can find people who want them," said Sara.

"You will," said Olivia. "Believe me, you will."

Mandy crossed her fingers that Olivia was right.

Back at the Grants' house, the puppies were wide awake. With Shan looking on, they were play-fighting in the nursery like miniature wrestlers.

"Could we stay for a while, please, Dad?" Mandy pleaded.

"Just for ten minutes," said Dr. Adam. "We're having dinner with Gran and Grandpa, remember?"

Alfie had been rolling around with Berkeley, but he suddenly ran to Sara and raised his paw, like he wanted her to shake it.

"You're such a smart puppy," Sara praised him, picking him up. He squirmed around in her arms and licked her face, then, seeing Mandy approaching, braced himself as if he was about to leap across to her.

"No, you don't." Sara chuckled, restraining him. "You might be smart, but you can't fly."

Sara handed him to Mandy. As she cuddled him, sadness filled her once more. *I hope you won't go blind*, she thought. And then into her mind came a picture of Neptune wearing his harness and chasing a scent across a wide-open field. "You're going to be just fine," she whispered to Alfie, "no matter what happens."

Dr. Adam had been standing at the door with Sara's parents, watching the puppy fun. He tapped his watch. "We really have to go now, Mandy and James."

"Before you do," said Mrs. Grant, "we have some important news."

Sara spun around. "We do?"

"Tulip, Berkeley, and Alfie have all found homes," announced Mr. Grant.

"They have? That's great," said Sara, and although she smiled, she looked disappointed, too. When she reached for Alfie and hugged him tightly to her, Mandy knew it was going to be very hard for Sara to give him up. "Who bought them?" Sara asked.

"Remember the Wilsons?" her dad asked.

"They're taking one!" exclaimed Sara. "After we insulted Rick like that?"

"He forgave you; his parents agreed it was only natural to go after any lead," said Mr. Grant. "Rick has been badgering them nonstop, ever since he heard about the puppies being at risk of developing PRA. He seems even more eager to have a dog that might need special help. He even got a job delivering vegetables on his bike so he can help pay for him."

"Him?" said Sara. She hugged Alfie closer. "Rick's chosen one of the boys?"

"Yes," said her dad. "He's taking Berkeley."

Sara closed her eyes momentarily, like she was relieved. "I'm really glad Rick's taking him," she said when she opened them again.

"Who's taking the other two?" asked James. Tulip tugged at the bottom of his jeans. He bent down to unhook her sharp teeth.

"That's one very lucky puppy," said Mrs. Grant. "We couldn't have asked for a better home. She's going to someone who knows all about blind dogs, and where there's also a big brother to keep her company."

Mandy took a wild guess. "Not Olivia Moult?"

"Exactly right!" said Mr. Grant. "We kept the news a surprise until you'd met her for yourselves."

"And Tulip won't be the only one to benefit," said Mrs. Grant. "Olivia said that a young dog will give Neptune a new lease on life as he gets older."

It was all working out better than Mandy could have dreamed. She crossed her fingers that Alfie would be going to a perfect home, too. "And Alfie?" Out of the corner of her eye, she saw Sara turn away as if she couldn't bear to hear that her favorite puppy was finally leaving home.

"With Alfie," said Mr. Grant, "there is a problem."

Sara whirled around to stare at her dad. "A problem?" she echoed.

"Uh-huh. The two of you are practically joined at the

hip. We would never be able to pry you apart, so . . ." Mr. Grant didn't get a chance to finish because Sara ran to him and threw herself and Alfie into his arms.

"He's really mine?" she said, laughing and crying at the same time.

"He's really yours," said her dad.

Mandy had to blink back her tears and she heard James sniff. Dr. Adam put his arm around her. "Time to go," he said, and as they left the puppy nursery he took a tissue out of his pocket and gave it to her. "You're a sorry sight," he said. "With all this sniffling going on, you'd think we were watching a tragedy."

Mandy wiped her eyes and glanced back into the room. Sara sat cross-legged on the floor with Alfie curled in her lap, while Shan, Tulip, Verona, and Berkeley tumbled around her. Mr. and Mrs. Grant stood arm in arm, laughing at the sight of Sara being mobbed by a pack of tiny yellow dogs.

"It could have been a tragedy," Mandy said thoughtfully. "But it turned out to be a doggy drama with the happiest ending ever!"